---

# WILD WITH YOU

---

*A Light My Fire Novel*

## J.H. CROIX

Cover design by Najla Qamber Designs

Cover Photography: Regina Wamba

Cover model: Jade McKenzee



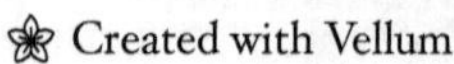 Created with Vellum

*"To love is to burn, to be on fire." -Jane Austen*

**Sign up for my newsletter for information on new releases & get a FREE copy of one of my books!**

*http://jhcroixauthor.com/subscribe/*

**Follow me!**

*jhcroix@jhcroix.com*

*https://amazon.com/author/jhcroix*

*https://www.bookbub.com/authors/j-h-croix*

*https://www.facebook.com/jhcroix*

*https://www.instagram.com/jhcroix/*

*Chapter One*

# MADISON

My corgi let out a sharp bark.

"What is it, Wilbur?"

My dog stared up at me, his dark brown eyes glinting with joy. He let out a softer woof before plunking his chunky little bottom on the ground by my feet. I looked ahead, and my breath caught in my throat. Mountains, trees, and a glittering lake stretched out in the view ahead.

"We're in Alaska," I whispered to Wilbur, almost reverently. I'd read things about beauty eliciting awe, but I'd never experienced it on a bone-deep level until now.

I'd driven away from Houston, Texas, a week and a half prior. I was definitely a city girl, but that was about to change in a *major* way. My life had blown up, and I needed somewhere to go. When I found out my grandfather, who'd passed away a full two years ago, had left me his hunting lodge in Alaska, I took it as a sign from the universe.

Actually, I might have taken that sign with a touch of annoyance. Less than a year ago, I'd loved my job as an actuary in my father's investment business. Some people thought numbers were boring, but I loved them. The simple, straightforward manner of numbers soothed the restless anxiety that had been churning inside me for as long as I could remember.

It didn't matter that I loved my job. It all went up in smoke when he got nailed for fraud. The good life-style I'd been accustomed to had been whisked away like a piece of tissue in the wind. My mother wasn't speaking to me because, apparently, she actually had the expectation I would cook the books on my father's behalf and somehow clean up the mess he'd created.

Whatever. I wasn't willing to do that, but at least I had somewhere to go.

While I'd driven through Canada to Alaska, I'd experienced wonderment at the raw and almost fierce beauty of the landscape with a glacial river glittering an otherworldly blue and snow blinding white in the sunshine on the mountain peaks. Some days, I saw few other vehicles.

I'd crossed the border from Canada only an hour ago. We were officially in Alaska. I pulled out my phone, eyeing that single bar of reception. When I tapped the screen open to check the map, I let out a breath of relief when it worked.

"Dammit," I muttered. I still had over seven hours to go to get to Willow Brook, Alaska.

Texas prided itself on being a big state, but it seemed small in comparison to Alaska. I imagined people here laughed at Texan slogans. The distance wasn't going to stop me. I had driven this far in my not-so-reliable car with only Wilbur, my very loyal dog, for company. He'd been practically vibrating with excitement this entire trip. He'd known our neighborhood in Houston by heart, so this was a true adventure for him.

"Come on, Wilbur," I said. "Let's keep on going."

A while later, I pulled off at a viewing spot on the highway. This one appeared to be official, but honestly, the entire highway could be considered a viewing spot. I let Wilbur take a bathroom break and thoroughly sniff the area before climbing back into my car. I started up my hatchback, relieved when the engine turned over. Only last year, I'd had a brand-new Mercedes Benz. I'd loved that car. It had hurt to let it go.

When my father's company and all of his personal funds were frozen, and I lost my job as a result, it was only after a few months of no payments that the bank had wisely pointed out I'd be better off trading it in for something much more affordable. I could get a job, I knew I could, but the stain of my father's fraud was clinging to me in Houston. I needed a fresh start and hoped Alaska would give it to me.

I still had no idea about finding work here, but I kept telling myself I could find something online. I pulled back out on the highway after watching a caravan of recreational vehicles pass by. These large RVs seemed to travel in clusters. Seeing them helped me feel not so alone. I wouldn't exactly call it traffic, but people were definitely making their way along this otherwise sparsely traveled highway through the middle of nowhere.

By the time I saw the gas station, just a gas station and nothing else, I had started to get worried as the needle for my gas tank crept closer and closer to the empty mark. There wasn't a soul here, but a sign on the door gave instructions on using the automated gas pumps and an arrow pointed at the restrooms behind the gas station.

I filled my car up and decided it was a good time to take Wilbur for his evening break and get him some food before we hit the road again. I was a little worried about where to stay. I'd made reservations at a hotel, but the sun was already slipping down the sky. I didn't want to be driving alone in the darkness out here.

"Come on, Wilbur," I called as I opened the door.

I never had to use a leash with him. He always came when he was called. He leaped out of the car, trotting his sturdy little body over to the faded and crushed grass in a field beside us. There were bleached fuchsia petals scattered on the ground. I could only imagine that whenever those flowers were in bloom, whatever they were, it was stunning.

Wilbur didn't pay much attention to the petals other than to mark them several times as he trotted around. We turned to walk back toward my car when I heard a snorting sound. Glancing in the direction of the snort, I saw a moose at the edge of the field. The large brown animal eyed me suspiciously, its antlers dark against the backdrop of the watercolor sunset. The sky was a swirl of tangerine, gold, and red. If my pulse hadn't been pounding out of control, I might've appreciated the beauty of the moment.

Wilbur let out a sharp bark and then took off as fast as his little legs could carry him toward the moose.

"Wilbur! No!" I started to chase after him, but a man's voice came from behind me.

"I wouldn't do that."

Turning back, I saw that a truck was now parked beside my car. The man gestured toward the moose.

"Moose aren't predatory, but it's close to mating season. Get over here. You've got enough time."

He was kind of bossy, and I felt a prickle of annoyance.

"But—" I sputtered.

"Listen, lady, I can't help you if we both get trampled."

While Wilbur ran in a mad dash toward the moose, I hurried over to the man. In a flash, he'd caught me by the elbow and tugged me between his truck and my vehicle.

"Your dog will be fine. He's pretty quick on his feet," he offered with a chuckle.

Turning, I watched Wilbur do what I called his spinning move. As he dashed toward the moose, he flipped low on the ground and reversed directions. He was acrobatic and lightning fast.

The man had opened his truck and all I got was a glimpse of rumpled brown curls before he reappeared with a gun. I gasped, but he ignored me and stepped past me, walking a short distance beyond the back of his truck. "Stay there," he ordered before simply lifting the gun and firing toward a grassy rise nearby.

At the sound, the moose looked our way. After a moment, the animal turned and trotted off. Still panicky inside, I looked around wildly for Wilbur only to discover he was already on his way back to me. His tongue flopped out of the side of his mouth as he ran, sheer joy radiating from him. His brown, black, and white body was vibrating when he stopped at my feet and sat. The man did something with the gun and then rounded to the other side of his truck to put it away.

I knelt, pulling Wilbur into my arms. "Oh, I'm so glad you're okay," I murmured. He was more than okay, wiggling like crazy and clearly of the mind that he had vanquished the giant moose all on his own.

"I'm glad you're both okay," the man said as I straightened and he reappeared between the vehicles.

I finally got my first good look at him. Holy smokes. Every cell in my body clambered up and shook itself off as if coming out of hibernation.

Alaska seemed to do everything in spades, and this man was an outsized, overblown version of masculinity. His rumpled brown curls were paired with starlight blue eyes, almost too bright for words. He had bold features with cheekbones sculpted sharply and a blade of a nose on the large size. All of him was on the large size, so it didn't even stand out. There was a little crook in it, and I couldn't help but wonder if he'd ever broken it. My eyes continued their exploration, noting the strong line of his jaw with a dimple at the chin and full sensual lips.

Because my eyes were greedy, they just kept on going, taking in the way his broad shoulders filled out his navy-blue Henley shirt. Although it was late summer and downright chilly this afternoon, his skin was bronzed in the vee where the shirt fell open at the top. I didn't doubt he was muscled all over with the way he filled out his clothes. His faded denim jeans were buttery soft and hugged his muscled thighs. My eyes landed on a pair of well-worn leather boots before he cleared his throat.

My eyes whipped up, colliding with his stunning blues. My breath caught in my throat, and I could hear the thundering beat of my pulse racing through my body.

"Hi, I'm Madison Glen." I thrust my hand out abruptly.

The man blinked, and I noticed he had thick curly

eyelashes. Good grief. This was almost too much. His lips twitched at the corners before one side lifted in a bemused grin, which sent my belly into several spinning flips. He reached out, almost lazily, and his big hand gripped mine and gave it a strong shake. His touch was warm and firm, and I could feel the calloused surface of his fingertips as he drew his touch away.

A handshake. A mere handshake, and I was *seriously* hot and bothered. Just now, I suddenly realized I'd never experienced feeling hot and bothered. Not that I had any doubts about the broken engagement I'd left back in Texas, but wow, what a relief that was over. I hadn't even known what I was missing. All I'd done was shake this man's hand, and heat had pervaded every corner of my body.

"Graham, Graham Holden. I take it you're not from around here."

I was *not* the kind of girl who got flustered. I swear, I was not. Aside from this being my first experience with hot and bothered, I was now officially flustered. I took a breath, albeit a shallow, fairly useless one that did absolutely nothing to slow the gallop of my pulse. "No, I'm not from here. I'm from Texas. This is Wilbur," I offered, gesturing down to my dog, who cheerfully smiled up at both of us.

If I thought things were bad already, then Graham knelt to give Wilbur a proper greeting. "Hey there, Wilbur."

Graham stroked over his head, and Wilbur was overjoyed, wagging his little tail and rubbing his head on Graham's knees. Meanwhile, my own knees were wobbly, and I thought I might legit swoon.

*Chapter Two*

# GRAHAM

I was honestly relieved to pet Wilbur. I needed some kind of distraction. Madison, this woman who seemed to have been dropped from the sky into Alaska, had a straight line to my libido. And, frankly, my libido was like a car left in the garage for over a decade. This engine hadn't turned over in a while, and now it was revving like mad.

I had some manners, though, so after greeting her ecstatically friendly dog, I straightened. "Nice to meet you and Wilbur. Moose can be cranky, especially this time of year. Might wanna be careful."

Madison blinked at me. That was a relief too, if only for a second. Her eyes were startlingly beautiful—a rich, clear green. A second passed when her lashes lifted again. She was so out of place here, I wasn't sure what to think. I knew the best thing for me was to let this be nothing more than this—a passing interaction at a gas station.

"Okay," she finally said.

Being near her had derailed my thoughts, and I'd actually forgotten what I said. The look on my face must've given it away because she added, "I'll be careful about moose if I see any again."

The next thing I knew, I was asking a question. I didn't need to be asking this woman questions. "Are you taking a trip by yourself?"

She blinked at me again, her eyes guarded. "Yeah," she said.

I knew her nonchalance was feigned, but this *really* was none of my business. She had glossy dark brown hair, twisted into something resembling a bun with a pen stuck through it on top of her head. She was about medium height with plenty of curves. I didn't want to admit it, but my eyes lingered on the way her T-shirt stretched across her breasts and the way her hips filled out her jeans.

Madison shivered and tugged her jacket closed in front as she stuffed her hands in her pockets. "Well, thanks for helping me. I'll just be on my way."

"Sure thing. Wilbur was probably more help than me. Take care and safe travels," I managed as I stepped back.

She let Wilbur into the passenger seat and climbed into her car. I watched as they drove away. I'd already filled my truck with gas, but I crossed the parking area and went to the back of the building to use the restroom. I could be a man and just take a piss in the field, but it was completely visible from the road, and I didn't want to be that kind of an asshole.

Only minutes later, I was back on the highway, heading to Willow Brook. Much as I wanted not to think about Madison Glen, my brain was mulling over that encounter. She didn't fit the profile for someone traveling alone in Alaska. I didn't know what she was doing, but I was more curious than I should be about her.

The sunset was showy tonight, leaving a last burst of orange and red and gold behind the mountains as the sun slipped out of view. I wondered if my daughter, Allie, was driving my parents crazy tonight. Probably not. Most of the time, she was a good kid, and she usually only got cranky with me.

A chuckle rustled in my throat. My daughter was a spitfire. She was two years into being a teenager, and I knew the next four years weren't going to be particularly easy. I loved her to pieces, though, and I'd do anything for her. She was staying with my parents for the weekend. If I pushed it on the drive, I could get home tonight, but by that point, she'd be sound asleep. I decided I might as well stop at a hotel.

My options were limited. When I saw the lights of a lodge glittering in the distance, I made the call to see if they had any rooms left. If this was at the height of summer, during the crush of tourist season, I wouldn't have any luck. But I could probably snag a room tonight.

I'd taken a trip up north to do some training. I'd just taken a job as the superintendent for an expansion hotshot firefighter crew in the Willow Brook area. I had some equipment to pick up in Fairbanks, and it was more affordable for me to make the drive than to fly and sort out shipping.

Not much later, after a friendly elderly couple assured me they had several rooms available, I was walking down the hallway to my room when I felt a prickle on the back of my neck. Reflexively, I glanced over my shoulder to see none other than Madison Glen walking down the hall.

Her eyes were on the floor as she walked along, and once again, my mouth got ahead of my brain. "Wow, I didn't expect to run into you again."

Madison's head whipped up, and it felt as if sparks shimmered in the air between us when her eyes met mine from a few feet away. "Oh! Hi. What are you doing here?"

"Getting a room," I offered. "I presume you're doing the same. That's what most people do at a place like this."

Madison actually pursed her lips and lifted her chin. I saw the fire flash in her eyes. Once again, my body sat up and took notice as a jolt of lust sizzled through me. I didn't know what it was about this woman, but she got to me. Big time. I honestly struggled to remember the last time I'd paid much attention to a woman. I was no monk, but I barely had time for a rushed breakfast these days. Being a single father didn't allow for much free time, nor did being a hotshot firefighter. Throw in the reality that I was a cynical man, and it all added up to zero time for romance.

Madison's lips curled into a smile. "Excellent point, Graham. I am here for the night."

"I'm glad you're not trying to drive in the darkness. It can dip below freezing at night now even though it's only August."

Jesus. Now, I sounded just like my daughter said —lecturey.

"I appreciate your concern. Nice to see you again," she offered politely. She opened the door to the room beside mine.

I didn't realize I was still staring until she lifted her hand in a little wave before she slipped into the room, and the door clicked shut.

After I let myself into my room and tossed my bag on the dresser, I decided to head down to the restaurant. There might be actual humans there. There were, but it was pretty quiet. I had a beer and a burger with fries at the bar and was headed back to my room when I saw Madison. Again.

She stopped in the hallway as I approached. She turned, and I felt as if she were assessing me when I came to a stop a few feet away. She cocked her head to the side, and for a second, just a flash, I thought I saw vulnerability flickering there. Then she bit her lip.

Fuck me. This girl and her perfectly straight teeth denting the plump cushion of her bottom lip sent fire sizzling through me. She took a step closer, and I could feel the voltage vibrating across the short distance separating us. "I have a question, Graham."

"Yes?" I prompted, my voice laced with a ragged edge.

None of this made sense, but I couldn't have walked away from her if my life depended on it.

"Can I kiss you?" She had a Southern drawl, and it slid over me like warm honey.

Okay, then. I didn't know what I'd expected her to ask, but it wasn't that. No matter how insane it seemed, I decided that kissing her was *exactly* what I should do. Because I would never see this woman again. Maybe desire had no place in my life, but I could kiss an absolutely gorgeous girl and walk away with a memory.

"Oh, sweetheart, I'll kiss you," I murmured, taking one stride and lifting a hand.

When my palm cupped her cheek, I could feel the heat simmering under my touch. I felt caught in a mist of fire. There was chemistry, and then there was *this*. We were fire in a bottle.

I slid my palm down, letting my thumb trail over the wild beat of her pulse. I was gratified to feel it, to sense that perhaps her reaction to me was as powerful and primitive as mine to her. I slipped my hand into the spill of her silky dark hair, cupping her nape as I watched the clear green of her eyes darken like a forest in the shade.

I took an incremental step closer and felt the soft curves of her against my chest. I was a hard man, and she was all warmth and lush heat.

She opened her mouth to say something—hell if I knew what—and I said, "Shh. You wanted a kiss."

At that, her lashes brushed against her cheeks as she took in a shaky breath. I watched those lashes lift once more and saw the flash of fire in her green eyes. She tilted her head upward and closed the distance between our mouths.

When her lips brushed mine, that voltage sizzled, firing out sparks that spun into the need tightening every cell in my body. With a low growl, I fit my mouth over hers. I didn't take it too fast, not just yet. This was just a kiss, but I intended to make it one she would never forget. Maybe I was cynical, maybe there hadn't been much room for desire in my life, and maybe it had been too long since I'd really wanted anyone, but I loved kissing. It was the prelude to everything, yet entirely its own act.

The plush give of her lips underneath mine was intoxicating. The audible hitch of her breath in her throat and the just barely-there gasp when I teased the seam of her lips with my tongue nearly undid me.

Time slowed, and I felt suspended in that fiery mist where nothing else mattered, nothing but a girl who I knew hardly anything about. I knew her name and that she was from Texas, but that didn't matter. I wanted her fiercely. When her tongue glided against mine like tender silk, I knew she kissed like a dream.

I didn't know how fast it happened, but somewhere along the way, I turned Madison against the wall as I devoured her mouth. One palm was pressed against the wall as I learned her—the way she flexed against me, and the way she made these little sounds in her throat that drove me fucking wild, each one the lash of a whip against my desire, driving it forward.

By the time we broke apart, I was desperate for air and gulping in ragged breaths, just as she did. When I brought my eyes to hers again, we stared at each other. I saw my shock reflected in hers. I didn't know what it was between us, but it was like nothing I'd ever felt. I couldn't even hide my fear because, holy hell, what *was* this?

It took every ounce of restraint and discipline I possessed to move away from the imprint of her soft curves against me. I released my palm where I cupped her nape, my fingers sliding through the silky locks as my hand fell away.

She blinked, giving her head a visible shake as she straightened. "Well, I asked for a kiss, and you delivered," she finally said, her tone almost wondering.

"Why did you ask me for a kiss?"

*Because I wanted to, and I'll never see you again.*

My own words echoed in my thoughts

Graham's eyes skated over my face. I was already plenty hot and bothered, but his intense, searching look sent a fresh shiver over the surface of my skin.

After several beats of my heart, his lips curled up at one corner in a grin that sent butterflies twirling in my belly. Holy smokes. This man knew how to set every cell in my body simmering with fire.

I wanted more—more kisses, more everything, more Graham.

"Well then, Madison Glen, I guess I won't be seeing you again."

"It's not likely," I replied, trying to sound nonchalant when I felt anything but inside.

Graham took a step closer again, and my breath quickened. He lifted a hand, cupping my cheek. His thumb traced a sensual swipe across my bottom lip. I didn't mean to do what I did next, but the urge was too powerful to resist. I nipped lightly at his thumb before he drew it away.

His eyes widened slightly, and a low laugh rustled in his throat. "I think we might be dangerous together, sweetheart."

I couldn't even formulate a reply. My brain cells had immolated.

"Good night," he added as he stepped back.

My cheek and bottom lip tingled with a fiery pleasure in the aftermath of his touch.

"Good night," I whispered the second I could move. Fumbling with the key card for my room, I hurried in, not even caring that I slammed the door behind me.

I pressed my back against it, trying to catch my breath and scrambling for my sanity. I lightly traced my fingertips over my lips, and I could've sworn sparks leaped against my skin. Sweet hell. That kiss itself was pure fire.

I lowered my hand, holding it over my heart, the rampaging beat thumping against my palm as I tried to catch my breath. That kiss had been a wild impulse. I'd seen Graham approaching me in the hallway and thought I could just eat him up. He was so delicious and sexy and just the kind of man who made me feel like he could take care of me. I had deeply underestimated the depth of chemistry between us. The voltage was still reverberating through my body.

Wilbur came trotting over as I tried to catch my breath and sniffed at my feet. I gave myself a shake before pushing away from the door. My knees wobbled a little as I walked toward my hotel bed and collapsed on it. He followed me, hopping onto the bed beside me.

"Well, that was crazy," I said to the ceiling.

The ceiling had nothing to offer in return. All things considered, though, it was an excellent ceiling for staring. My eyes followed the grain of the wood. Although the ceiling didn't have anything to say, Wilbur offered a soft woof at my musings.

I tried to remember the last time I'd kissed anyone. It was over a year ago or thereabouts. Back when I thought my stupid fiancé, Dirk, had actually loved me. It was funny how much could shift in a single year. Dirk's kisses had never been all that satisfying. They'd been okay, but I'd told myself the rest of our relationship was great.

Ha! It wasn't great. It was about as deep as a puddle when all was said and done. Dirk wanted nothing to do with me when my father's connections started drying up along with my money.

I was chronically anxious about my current financial insecurity. More than that, though, I was ashamed of the person I'd once been. I couldn't even hold our breakup against Dirk because I'd probably been as shallow as him.

Graham had just given me the best kiss I'd ever had in my life. I laughed to myself and kicked off my shoes as I rolled up into a sitting position. My body was still tingling. The reverberations from the fiery jolt of that kiss were still pinging through my system.

I didn't have a ton of courage when it came to men. I'd thought maybe it would be fun to kiss Graham because I would never see him again, so it didn't matter if the kiss was a disaster. It didn't matter at all what he thought of me. And it had totally been worth it.

I glanced toward the wall between our rooms, realizing we might be sitting only a few feet apart. Awareness hummed to life in my body like a cluster of fireflies in the darkness. I didn't have the nerve to do more than kiss Graham.

All I knew was his name. Abruptly, I stood from the bed and crossed over to where my laptop sat on the dresser. I fetched it and returned to the bed. I started to enter his name in the search bar, and my hands fell still. I wasn't going to see him again. I didn't need to figure out who he was. He would be a memory for me—the best kiss. Ever.

I fell asleep that night, resolving to leave early in the morning. As much as I told myself not to, I couldn't help but wonder if I would see Graham before I left.

———

I didn't. See Graham, that is. I had a restless night of sleep, so I didn't even have to make an effort to get up early. I'd always been an early bird, but I felt as if I'd been chasing a good night's sleep for months now. I would wake up with thoughts churning through my mind, worrying about all the things I could do absolutely nothing about, much less in the lonely hours of darkness.

Nighttime worrying was so unforgiving. The mind could be ruthless at night, kicking open doors into the past that were supposed to stay shut and opening imaginary pathways into worries about a future that didn't even exist yet.

The sun was barely making its presence known when I walked out of the hotel. My breath frosted the air, and a thin line of silvery gold shimmered along the edge of the mountain range in the distance, almost as if offering a gateway between this world and another.

I took a breath of the bracing, crisp morning air and walked to my car, tossing my bag in the back seat and crossing over to the identified dog area. Wilbur did his business while the car warmed up. It was nice and toasty by the time I turned onto the road while he sat happily beside me in the passenger seat.

I drove south, watching the sunrise's spectacular explosion of color from the east. That thin line of light widened with layers of orange, red, and gold mingling as the sun rose higher and higher in the sky before finally cresting above the mountains.

I felt like nature should have a drum and bugle corps for a sunrise like that. I passed a highway sign indicating Willow Brook was only a few hours away.

My stomach tightened with anxiety. I'd never even been to Alaska, much less to my late grandfather's hunting lodge. When my mother had been dismissive and scoffed at my idea to move up here, I contacted the executor of my grandfather's estate and confirmed the home had all the amenities. According to my grandfather's attorney, it was entirely self-sufficient and generated by a combination of wind and solar power. He'd sent photographs, and it looked nice.

Nice or not, I was nervous, really nervous. My whole life had blown up, and I was trying to find somewhere to land. Maybe it was crazy, but I figured at least I had somewhere to go.

"We're getting closer, Wilbur."

My little corgi wiggled in his seat, casting me what I thought was a smile, but then he was generally cheerful. That was a good thing because lately, it felt as if he was my only friend. I supposed he was.

It was not pleasant to have life rip the foundation out from under your feet. In the span of months, I'd lost my job, my home, and the support of my family.

A few hours later, after a stop to fill my tank with gas in Anchorage and to give Wilbur another bathroom break, I saw the exit for Willow Brook—the place that was about to become my home. I followed the signs to "downtown" and actually smiled to myself. A warm sense of joy spun through me as I turned onto Main Street and saw the cute downtown area with shops and brightly colored signs. I smiled again as I passed Firehouse Café with bright red lettering on the sign and a cheery flag with flowers on it flapping in the wind. I'd been imagining that I would truly be in the middle of nowhere. While this was definitely far more wilderness than what I was accustomed to in Houston, obviously, there was a town here with all the amenities. There was a grocery store, a police and fire station, and even a sign for a hospital.

I had put the address given to me by my grandfather's attorney into my phone GPS and simply followed what it said. After I drove through downtown, things thinned out. There were driveways and roads, but the houses weren't crowded together here, that was for sure. Sometimes, I would go a few miles before I saw another driveway. When my friendly GPS told me where to turn onto Firefly Lane, it felt like I was far away from downtown even though only ten minutes had elapsed.

"You can handle this," I murmured to myself and Wilbur.

Wilbur wagged his chubby little tail, and I took that as a sign that I could, in fact, handle this. An unmarked gravel driveway was where my GPS told me to turn. There was a mailbox, but it looked drunk and was tilting to the side. There was snow on the mountain peaks in the distance. My mind was spinning as I realized I had tons of things to deal with. For example, there was no way I could shovel a driveway this long. I'd have to find someone to plow, and I knew absolutely no one here.

"You can handle this," I repeated to myself.

The driveway was roughly half a mile long. It ended in a circle, and there sat the house I recognized from the photos. It was a low-slung house, almost nestled into the trees surrounding it on a sloping hillside. The timber-frame structure had a bright green steel roof with an attached garage to the side.

I came to a stop and turned the engine off. I sat there as that soft ticking sound quieted while the engine cooled. Anxiety spun in my chest and stomach, and my heart was pounding out a rapid, staccato beat.

"Well, it's now or never," I said to Wilbur as I opened the glove compartment and fetched the key kept there in a small tin container.

Wilbur hopped out of the car after me and immediately began investigating the area. I was about to let him stay outside when I recalled our incident with the moose at that gas station. I could imagine Graham's disapproving look when he first gave me his little lecture about safety.

"Come on, Wilbur," I called.

He peed on a tree and immediately trotted up the stairs onto the wide porch that ran the length of the house. There were two rocking chairs on the porch. I turned to look behind me, and my breath caught in my throat. The house sat on a rise, offering a view of the mountains in the distance and a lake glittering under the sun.

It was easier to avoid getting caught up in the spinning wheels of worry, recrimination, and regret when the natural beauty knocked me off that track. Turning back to the door, I slid the key in the lock, letting out a breath I hadn't even known I'd been holding when the bolt smoothly slid open.

We stepped inside, and Wilbur promptly set out to

explore. The sound of his claws clicking on the hardwood floor echoed as I looked around. The home was furnished, but it had the feel of a space where no one had been in a long time. According to the attorney, my grandfather hadn't been here since he got sick and went into long-term care two years ago.

The furniture was covered in cloth drapes. I took a quick walk around. The front door opened into a tiled entryway with closets on either side. A wide archway led into what appeared to be the main living space. Windows covered the wall on the opposite side, offering a view of a field and trees. The field was covered in those fallen flowers with smudges of faded fuchsia covering the ground amidst a cluster of birch and spruce trees.

A stone fireplace was on one side of the living room, and bookshelves lined the other. All the shelves were empty at the moment. Another archway to one side led to the kitchen, which had counters on three sides and a small round table by another window. The appliances appeared fairly new, which kind of surprised me.

On the other side of the living room, a hallway led to three bedrooms. The bathroom in the hallway contained the laundry. I was surprised to find a lovely master bathroom with a soaking tub, complete with a window offering another pretty view.

I clasped my hands together, smiling as I looked around. My life might feel uncertain with the ground shifting under my feet, but I had a comfortable home.

I hurried back outside, moved my car into the garage, and brought in what few belongings I had. All I'd brought were my clothes, my toiletries, and Wilbur's things.

Wilbur happily curled up in his bed, and I decided

I might as well venture into town to get some groceries. I wasn't going to have tons of spending money until I found a new job, but I'd use my savings to stock up. Without needing to pay rent, my savings would stretch further and buy me some time.

The lawyer had already switched the utilities over to me. He'd also given me the name of the person who'd checked on the house periodically. By the time I returned from the grocery store, I was feeling accomplished.

I thought I could actually do this. I was pleasantly surprised to discover I had good cell reception here, so I could use my streaming subscription on my computer. Things were falling into place, at least for the night. All was well. Until someone started pounding on my front door that night.

## Chapter Four

# GRAHAM

*Six hours earlier*

I walked down the hallway at Willow Brook Fire & Rescue. I passed an office, slowing when I heard someone call my name. Taking a few steps back, I peered through the doorway.

"Hey, man," Cade Masters said from where he sat at a small round table with Beck Steele and Levi Phillips.

Cade was a superintendent for one of the hotshot crews here, and Beck and Levi were also hotshot firefighters. I'd known them all for years, seeing as I'd grown up in the area. I'd started here as a town firefighter and recently taken the position as superintendent on the new expansion hotshot crew.

"What's up?" I asked, leaning my shoulder inside the doorframe.

"Just wondering how your trip went. Any trouble picking up that equipment?" Cade asked.

"Nope. No problem. Some of the guys just helped

me carry it into the storage area. I thought I'd pop over to let your dad know his stuff is in there."

Cade flashed a grin. "He'll appreciate it."

Rex Masters was the town's police chief and Cade's father. We shared this building with the town's police force.

Beck asked, "Did you get my special vest?"

Levi chuckled. "Special vest?"

Beck nodded. "We're all getting new vests."

Cade simply rolled his eyes while I shrugged. "I'm the delivery guy. That's it. Feel free to go paw through the boxes," I added, thumbing over my shoulder in the direction down the hall where the storage area was.

Beck stood from the table. "I'm going now. I love new stuff."

I pushed away from the doorframe and stepped back into the hallway, making room for Beck to pass by. "I'll catch you guys tomorrow. I gotta hit the store and make sure I've got some food at home after I check in with your dad."

With a wave, I headed toward the front of the station. A moment later, I pushed through the doorway into the reception and dispatch area which was situated between the fire station and the police station. Maisie Steele, Beck's wife, stood from the desk. She was the main dispatcher for the town. Her brown curls bounced when she smiled over at me as she finished a call. "All right, we'll have one of the officers head out there and check for you."

She hung up as I paused at the round counter encircling her desk. "Sounds like a call for the police?" At her nod, I added, "I hate when I'm not on duty, and there's a call for the crew."

Her big brown eyes crinkled at the corners with

her smile. "I think you're all like that. It's that rescue complex."

"Rescue complex?"

She shrugged lightly. "Yeah. Beck has the same issue."

I'd been surprised when Beck got married. He'd gone from being a total flirt to a completely committed family man with two kids.

"We just like doing our jobs. Anyway, you've got a bunch of office supplies that came with everything else I picked up in Fairbanks. Thought you might wanna know. Beck beat feet in there because apparently, he likes new stuff," I said dryly.

Maisie shook her head and laughed softly. "He does. He's like a kid. Thanks for getting those supplies for me."

"No problem. I was going anyway." I tapped my fingers on her desk as I pushed away. "Catch you later."

She waved as she sat down and took another call for dispatch. I pushed through the swinging door into the police side of the building. Rex was taking a call, but he hung up when I peered into his office. He and Cade looked remarkably alike. Rex was more weathered, with deep laugh lines around the corners of his green eyes. Leaning back in his chair, he ran his fingers through his brown and silver curls.

"What's up?" he asked.

"Just stopping in to let you know your stuff is in the storage area."

Rex nodded. "All right, good to know. Thanks again. You saved us some money by not having to ship it down here."

"Happy to help. Catch you later. I'll be in tomorrow because I'm on duty."

Rex's phone was already ringing as I stepped back, lifting my hand in a quick wave. I headed down the hallway, returning to the parking area. After a quick stop at the grocery store, I figured I'd grab some pizza to go.

Walking into Alpenglow Pizza a while later, I ran into Levi with his wife, Lucy. In all honesty, Lucy intimidated the hell out of me. Although she was petite, she was fierce. That said, she smiled when Levi greeted me for the second time today. "Hey, man, sounds like you had the same idea we did."

"Pizza to go?" I returned as I stopped beside them.

"Yep. This pizza is freaking amazing," Levi added.

"Sure is."

"How's everything out at your place?" Levi asked as the line inched forward.

"Pretty good. I need to make some repairs, though." I glanced at Lucy. "Do you and Amelia do small projects?"

"We do anything," she replied.

Along with Cade's wife, Amelia, Lucy ran Kick-Ass Construction. It had the best reputation in town as far as construction companies went.

"Perfect. I can do the work myself, but I don't have time. I'll stop by and chat with you two at some point. Maybe next spring, though. I'd like to say I could get it done before winter, but it ain't happening. Are you all booked up?"

"We're always busy," she offered with a quick shrug. "For smaller jobs, we can usually find a way to fit things in. Beck knows our office number."

By then, they were at the front of the line. "I'll call next spring when I have time to plan."

In short order, I was headed home with a large pizza. Allie and I wouldn't finish it tonight, but left-over pizza was the best. As I was driving home, I idly noticed there were lights on at Harold's old place. He hadn't been here in years and had passed away. I was curious if the place had sold recently.

When I got home, my daughter, Allie, was waiting for me. "Hey, Dad!" She threw her arms around my neck, and I squeezed her tight with my free arm for a second before she bounced away.

"Ooh, you got pizza!"

I grinned. "Sure did. You hungry?"

Allie shrugged, and her brown curls bounced with the motion. "Kinda. Gram had a snack for me after school, but I still want pizza."

I walked past her after toeing my boots off and aimed for the kitchen. "Well, let's eat."

A few minutes later, I was just about to bite into my pizza when my cell phone rang. I was surprised to see Rex Masters' name flash on the screen. I swiped my thumb across the screen. "What's up, Rex?"

"I was wondering if you minded swinging by and checking on Harold's place. We've had two calls that the lights are on there. I don't want to assume it's a break-in, but he hasn't been here in at least two years. Janet James was checking on the place, but she's out of town tonight. I left her a message but haven't heard back."

"I'll drive over right now," I said.

"Thanks. Give me a call if I need to drive out there. You're right next door, so I figured I'd ask you first."

I took a quick bite of pizza to stave off my hunger pangs. Allie looked up when I stood from the table. "Where are you going?"

"Rex wants me to check on the place next door. Be right back."

Allie nodded and took another bite of pizza. Minutes later, I rolled to a stop in Harold's driveway. Before he passed away, Harold was what was known as a snowbird in Alaska. He built his home for hunting and spent summers here, but he left every winter. Roughly two years ago, he'd called to let me know he was having health problems and had moved into a long-term care facility.

Glancing around the small circle at the end of the driveway, I studied the closed garage. With the lights on, I presumed whoever was here was parked in the garage. I climbed out of my truck and walked up the stairs. I knocked on the door, wondering who was here.

A moment later, I heard a sharp bark. I hoped whoever was about to open the door didn't have an asshole of a dog. The door swung open, and my chin might've hit the floor. Madison Glen stood there.

Unsettled and rattled by my body's instantaneous jolt of lust, I led with, "Breaking and entering?"

Madison's eyes flashed, and she put a hand on her hip. "Absolutely not. I own this place."

Annoyance prickled through me. "I know you don't own this place. It's owned by Harold Brady. He passed on a few years ago, but as far as I know, it hasn't sold."

Madison let out a heavy sigh. "Harold was my grandfather, and he willed me his place after he passed away."

"Bullshit," I countered as Wilbur trotted out and circled my feet.

"Wilbur! Don't be nice to him," Madison ordered.

I looked down at the dog with his stub of a tail wagging. I leaned over to stroke my palm down his back. Straightening, I ignored the way the hairs stood on my body, attenuating to Madison's presence as a hum of desire coursed through me. "Harold used to come here every year. I knew him well because I live next door." I gestured to the trees.

Madison's gaze followed the direction of where I pointed. "In the trees?" she returned, her tone tart.

I rolled my eyes when she looked back at me. "No. Not in the trees. Through those trees is another house. Harold specifically said he didn't have any family, if you're wondering why I'm doubting you." I was feeling downright mulish about Madison's presence here.

"Well, he lied. He also wasn't on speaking terms with my mother, who was his daughter."

A chilly breeze gusted through the trees, and Madison's eyes narrowed. "It's cold. Am I free to remain in the house I own?" she pressed, her tone dripping with sarcasm.

"Look, I need to call the police."

"What?!" she squeaked.

"I didn't come here because I'm nosy. The police chief asked me to check on the house."

"Oh, my God. You've got to be freaking kidding me," she muttered. "Whatever, come here, Wilbur." She snapped her fingers, and he immediately stopped circling my feet and trotted to her.

"Can I come in?" I asked as I slipped my phone out of my pocket.

"What? You're accusing me of breaking and entering. Why would I invite you in?"

"I'm calling the police chief to sort this out."

Madison's expression was mutinous, but she stepped back from the door and gestured for me to enter. Walking through, I closed the door behind me. Madison crossed her arms tightly and waited under the archway that led from the entry area into the living room. She tapped her foot on the floor, although the effect was ruined by the fact she wore fluffy socks, pink with dogs on them, an incongruent touch to the princess vibe she gave off.

A second after I called, Rex answered, "What's up?"

"There's a woman here, Madison Glen. She claims Harold was her grandfather. I told her I didn't think that was the case because he said he didn't have any family."

Rex's sigh filtered through the line. "Janet would know, so let me keep trying to reach her."

"What do you want me to do about Madison?"

"Do you mind waiting?" Rex asked.

"Well, she clearly doesn't want me here."

Rex chuckled. "Well, I guess if she takes off after you leave, then we've solved our problem."

"True story. After you get ahold of Janet, give me a call and let me know what she says."

Hanging up, I lifted my eyes to Madison's again. "That was the police chief. He's going to ask the woman who checked on the place periodically. She's out of town, so he's waiting to hear back."

Madison rolled her eyes. Without a word, she turned and stalked away, disappearing down the hallway to one side. Wilbur followed her. Unsure what to do, I waited. They returned a few moments later, and Madison thrust some paperwork at me.

Glancing down, I skimmed it. It appeared to be a will and the deed to this house. I brought my eyes to hers again. "None of us knew Harold had any family. Alaska is an easy place for people to disappear, and I already know you're from out of town."

Madison's lips pressed in a line. She snatched the

paperwork back from me, her fingers brushing mine and sending heat sizzling in the wake of her glancing touch.

"Fine. Could you please leave?"

Sweet Jesus. Her haughty tone and the icy look in her eyes set every cell in my body on fire. I didn't know what it was about this woman, but holy freaking hell, she turned me on.

"I'll leave, but I'm sure the police chief will be following up."

"Whatever." She waved airily as if she were dismissing me. "Just go."

I took a last look at her and turned on my heel. When the door clicked shut behind me, I hesitated for a beat before forcing my feet to walk down the stairs and to my truck.

A few minutes after I returned home, my phone rang. "It's Rex!" Allie called.

"I'll take it."

I'd filled her in when I got back from my brief visit with Madison. Allie was excited about the potential for a new neighbor, and she'd been waiting for Rex to call.

I answered, "What's the scoop?"

"Madison Glen *is* Harold's granddaughter. He wasn't on good terms with her mother, but he left everything to Madison," Rex explained. "You officially have a new neighbor."

A few hours later, I laid in bed, fiery hot memories of that kiss with Madison spinning through my thoughts on repeat. She lived next door. This was going to be interesting.

## Chapter Five

# GRAHAM

"Allie, come on!"

"I'm coming!" she called in return.

My daughter pounded down the stairs, practically skidding to a stop in the kitchen as she came around the corner.

"Can we get coffee?" she asked.

I arched a brow. "Coffee?"

Allie shrugged, her blue eyes twinkling. "Yes." I waited. She rolled her eyes. "Okay. Not coffee. Hot chocolate," she amended because she knew coffee for her wasn't on the menu.

When she saw the look on my face, she added, "I just want to stop by Firehouse Café. I'd like one of those cranberry orange scones too. Please."

Aw, hell. I couldn't say no, even if I wanted to, so I nodded. "Can do."

"Yay!"

Glancing at my watch, I added, "We need to roll. You only have a half an hour before school starts."

Allie's curls bounced on her shoulders as she spun away and hurried toward the entryway. I heard the rustle of her backpack as she yanked it out of the closet. I grabbed my keys and wallet off the counter and followed her outside.

As we began the drive into town, she commented, "Do you think our new neighbor will be nice?"

I'd kept it vague last night, but she must've seen the smile teasing at the corners of my mouth.

"What else do you know?" she chirped.

"I told you it was Harold's granddaughter last night," I replied, briefly sliding my gaze to hers before looking at the road again. I shook my head, almost to myself. "I didn't even know he had a granddaughter."

"I knew he had a granddaughter."

"You did?"

"Yeah."

"Are you serious? I talked to him every year when he came, and he never mentioned a granddaughter. In fact, he made a point of making it clear that he didn't have any family."

Allie looked awfully pleased with herself when I glanced over as I came to a stop before turning onto the highway. She pursed her lips and shrugged. "You talked to him about guy things, hunting and stuff. He told me about the rest. He doesn't stay in touch with his family, or he didn't." A shadow passed through her eyes, and she looked away.

My daughter bonded tightly to people. Harold had doted on her, and she'd loved it. When she looked out the window, I turned onto the highway that would lead us into Willow Brook.

"His granddaughter, Maddie, is the only one he kept in touch with. He hoped she wouldn't turn out like his daughter. He didn't like his daughter," Allie offered.

"No?"

I didn't like how curious I was about Madison or Maddie, as Harold apparently referred to her. I hoped for once my usually chatty fourteen-year-old would offer up whatever she knew. She didn't need to know that I'd crossed paths with Madison before. She certainly didn't need to know the woman had nearly set me on fire. I was still feeling the occasional reverberation from that kiss. It felt as if cinders had settled inside me in its aftermath, and the embers of the fire still burned.

Allie kept on talking. "I don't know all the details. All I know is he thought his daughter was a money-grubber, and she married an asshole. He told me he planned to leave his place to his granddaughter. We haven't seen her since he passed away, so I thought maybe she didn't want it."

"She does," I offered.

Allie snorted. "I bet that was funny, you showing up and checking on the place, and it's actually hers. Did you do your whole firefighter-take-care-of-the-world thing?"

"What are you talking about?" I countered.

"Your vibe, always taking care of everybody. That's all."

"It's my job," I muttered.

"You're not a cop," she pointed out.

"No, but Rex asked me to stop by and check on the place, like I told you last night," I returned just as pointedly.

"I can't wait to meet her. Can I go over after school today?"

"I don't know. She might not want surprise guests."

Allie sighed heavily. She'd perfected the art of sighing. As of late, every sigh was imbued with shades of meaning, all of which I was supposed to intuit even if she didn't elaborate.

"We're her neighbors. She'll feel all alone and unwelcome. Plus, you went by acting like you were a cop," she added.

"I made sure to tell her I was not a cop and explained that Rex asked me to stop by and check on the place." I felt more defensive than I wanted to. Lately, my daughter had the unique ability to elicit a sense of defensiveness over the most minor things.

"I'll take you over there this weekend. How's that?"

Allie bounced her heels on the floorboard. "That'd be great."

I turned onto Main Street, watching as golden leaves scudded across the road in front of us. We were headed into autumn, and the leaves were starting to fall from the birch and cottonwood trees. Most of the forests around Willow Brook were evergreen, but there were clusters of birch and cottonwood.

We drove past Willow Brook Fire & Rescue, and the parking lot was noticeably full. Rex was probably having a meeting over on the police side, or one of the other crews was having a staff meeting. The sign for Firehouse Café appeared ahead, its bright red lettering announcing the town's favorite—and only—coffee shop. Other places served coffee, but it wasn't the main draw. I couldn't imagine anyone even trying to compete with Firehouse Café.

Moments later, I'd parked, and Allie was already hurrying out of the truck. "We don't have time to hang out," I called as I caught up to her.

"I know, Dad. My first class starts in twenty minutes. That gives us ten minutes here, five minutes to the school, and five minutes for me to get in the building and to class. Plenty of time." She tapped her watch for emphasis.

Chuckling, I followed her in the café. The scents of fresh coffee and baked goods filled my senses. Allie skipped to the line and tapped the shoulder of a man waiting.

He glanced back, a smile cracking open on his face. "Well, hey, Allie." Beck's eyes lifted to mine. "Good to see you, Graham. How're you two doing this morning?"

"I'm getting a cranberry orange scone before school," Allie whispered conspiratorially.

Beck nodded solemnly. "Good call. You should get two and sneak one into class."

I rolled my eyes. "Seriously, dude."

Beck flashed a grin. "Sorry. I always snuck food in school. You did too."

I sighed. "I know. I just don't want her to get in trouble the way I did. She's a straight-A student."

"Fair enough. Don't do what your dad and I did," Beck added, pulling one of Allie's curls and letting it go with a bounce.

He was next in line, and Allie prodded him in the back when the couple in front of him stepped out of the way. "Hurry up. I have a time limit, or I'll be late for school."

"Go ahead. I can wait." Beck gestured for us to step in front of him.

"You don't mind?" I asked.

"Nah." He shook his head quickly.

"I'll cover your coffee then. You getting a shot in the dark?"

Beck nodded.

"Did you do that just so Dad would buy your coffee?" Allie asked pointedly.

Beck threw his head back with a laugh. "Nah, I'm not that slick. Honestly, I just wanted you to make it to school on time. I can be chatty. Janet knows that."

Janet smiled amongst the three of us. "That I do," she agreed. "What'll it be?"

"Can I get two cranberry orange scones and—" Allie began.

"No coffee," I cut in.

Janet chuckled. "You're too young for coffee, dear." Allie groaned.

"Hot chocolate is what you want, right?" I pressed.

Allie brightened instantly with an enthusiastic nod. I ordered Beck's and my coffee, and we stepped out of the way to wait while Janet prepped everything. "Heard you have a new neighbor," she commented.

"We do. It's Harold's granddaughter. Do you know her?"

"I met her this morning. She's right over there." Janet pointed toward the windows to the side of the café.

All three of us swiveled to look where she pointed. Madison sat at a table. Sunshine was falling through the window, creating shimmery glints of gold amidst her dark locks. She was stunning.

Allie swung to me, her eyes wide. "Can I go meet her?"

"You can't be late for school," I warned.

"I won't." Allie didn't wait before she skipped across the café as Janet chuckled.

"You can be grateful your teenager isn't sullen and hates to talk to adults," she offered encouragingly.

I'd known Janet for as long as I could remember. Growing up in Willow Brook, I had memories of my parents bringing me here when she owned the place with her late husband. He passed away after an acci-dent on an icy highway, and she carried on with her warm smile, her kind brown eyes, and her familiar dark hair streaked with silver that she almost always wore in a braid. She felt like a grandmother to me.

"I know I'm lucky," I replied. "She's a good kid." My eyes flicked to Beck. "Can you grab our stuff when it's ready?"

He nodded. "You got it. I'll bring it over."

Crossing the small café, I tried to ignore the subtle buzz of electricity that set to thrumming in my body. When I stopped by the table, I caught the tail end of my daughter's comment.

"I live next door with my dad. He's the one who pretended to be a cop and showed up asking who you were," Allie explained.

Stopping beside the table, I glanced at Allie and shrugged. "I stopped by because Rex asked me to. Did you introduce yourself?"

"Of course, I might have forgotten to tell you my name, though. I'm Allie, Allie Holden. This is my dad. He's a hotshot firefighter. He's nice, although he probably seemed a little bossy when he acted like you were a criminal."

Madison's eyes swung to mine. I felt a little jolt, as if a tiny bolt of lightning struck me, when her pretty green eyes collided with mine. Her face was fresh and pink-cheeked. She had this sultry, wholesome vibe that confused me. She was almost too pretty for it.

I tried to tell myself I needed to give her more of a chance. It's just she reminded me too much of Allie's mother, who was long gone. She'd been mostly absent from Allie's life since a month after she was born.

"Hi, Graham," Madison said, dipping her head.

"Do you go by Madison or Maddie?" Allie interjected.

Madison's lips twitched at the corners. "Both, so take your pick."

"I go by Allie, even though my name is Alison," Allie offered.

"Do you answer to Alison?" Madison asked.

Allie pursed her lips, tapping her fingertip on her cheek. "Sometimes. Dad only calls me that when he's frustrated."

Madison's eyes lifted to mine, and I saw the mirth glinting there.

As I fought the urge to grin, Beck arrived. "Here are your scones. Don't get yourself in trouble if you try to sneak one in class," he offered as he handed the small paper bag to Allie.

I glanced at him, adding, "Karma. You just wait. Once your oldest is fourteen, you'll think twice about encouraging them to behave the way we did when we were in high school," I teased as he handed me my coffee.

Beck's eyes widened. "Dude, I'm not ready. Don't give me a heart attack."

With a low laugh, I gestured to Madison. "This is Madison Glen. She's Harold's granddaughter who inherited his old place." Pointing at Beck, I added, "This is Beck Steele. We grew up together, and he's also a hotshot firefighter here in town."

Beck dipped his chin in acknowledgment. "Nice to meet you, and welcome to Willow Brook. We all loved Harold even though he wasn't around very much."

Madison's lips tightened at the corners, and an intense emotion flashed through her eyes before she shuttered it quickly. "He meant a lot to me. I didn't know he'd left me his place until a few months ago. I'm glad to know people here cared about him. I didn't get to see as much of him as I wanted," she offered.

I was way too freaking curious about Madison. I wanted to know why Harold disowned Madison's mother. But if Harold was close to Madison, then she couldn't be all that bad. That said, family could overlook all kinds of stuff. Hell, I'd given Allie's mother the benefit of the doubt for way too long when it came to Allie.

"We need to get you to school," I interjected.

Allie let out a put-upon sigh. "Fine." Her eyes bounced to Madison. "Can I come over and visit this weekend, Maddie?"

Madison's eyes shifted to mine. At my nod, she replied, "Sure. Let me give you my number."

She pulled out her phone, and I watched as my daughter exchanged numbers with a woman who pretty much set my body on fire. Just being near her again had heat rising swiftly inside me, sparking the electricity sizzling through my veins.

"You sure that's okay?" I couldn't help but ask.

Madison nodded. "Of course, I don't know anyone in town except you three now and Janet over at the counter. Friendly neighbors are a good thing. I have an excessively friendly dog. Your dad may have mentioned him."

Allie's eyes snapped to mine. "What? You didn't mention she had a dog."

"I didn't think about it," I replied sheepishly.

Allie huffed. "I have to go to class. I can't wait to meet your dog."

A few minutes later, we were back in my truck. "How could you forget about her dog?" Allie asked, her tone accusatory.

"I just didn't think of it."

The question of a dog had been on the radar for the last year. Allie's beloved childhood dog, Banana, had passed away, and she wanted another one. We didn't have time for training a puppy, so I'd been putting it off. Now that Madison lived next door with a dog, I knew this meant plenty more discussion on the matter.

"We can talk about the possibility of a dog at another time," I added.

Allie shrugged. "Fine. Maddie's really pretty, by the way."

I slid my eyes sideways. My way too perceptive daughter had likely sensed my reaction to Madison. Fuck my life.

## Chapter Six

# MADISON

I was waiting at the counter for a coffee to go before I left. Janet, who'd introduced herself when I came in, was peering through the waist-high door into the kitchen behind her and replying to something an employee said.

I took a moment to glance around. The café was cute and inviting. The tall, square brick building had an open, airy space for dining in what apparently used to be the town's fire station. Beyond the counter, the kitchen was visible with scents of baked goods and coffee pervading the entire café. The old fire pole was painted with bright pink flowers, adding a touch of whimsy. The windows let plenty of light in and offered a view of the cute downtown shopping area.

Janet turned back and began getting my coffee ready. "I hope it didn't freak you out to have Graham check on the place last night."

Before I could respond, she added, "Graham's a good guy, if a little, well, prickly."

"That's one way to put it," I replied. "I thought he was going to arrest me."

Janet chuckled. "Graham would not have arrested you. Rex Masters—he's the police chief—had left me a message, but I didn't even notice because I was busy. By the time I called Rex back to confirm you were Harold's granddaughter and had inherited the property, he had already asked Graham to stop by because he lives next door. At least you know we look after each other around here. Are you planning to stay?"

Janet was curious and didn't even try to hide it. She was also really nice, and I could use a few more nice people in my life. "For the time being, I plan to stay. I can work online, so I'm hoping I can find some opportunities here. Maybe in Anchorage."

"What do you do?"

"I'm an actuary."

Janet gave me a long look. "Wow, that sounds terrifically difficult and maybe boring."

I laughed. "To some people. I love numbers. They relax me. I know it's weird, but it is what it is."

Janet chuckled. Her eyes twinkled with her smile. I'd liked her instantly. She was warm and funny and welcoming. She gave off a motherly vibe, and I sensed she was protective of those she cared about.

While I felt instantly comfortable with her, I internally shook my head at myself. I was so filled with doubts about myself. This past year of my life had left me feeling exposed and stripped bare, as if the façade of a house had been torn off to reveal it was nothing more than a stage prop.

"Graham can be grumpy," Janet offered, "but he's got a heart of gold."

She counted out my change and handed it over with my coffee to go. "He's got his hands full with Allie. She's a little firecracker, that girl."

"How old is she?"

Janet drummed her fingertips on the edge of the counter. "Fourteen. Graham's been a single father since only a month after she was born."

"Really?"

Janet nodded, brushing her braid off her shoulder. "Allie's mother was his high school girlfriend. She was a looker. There's no doubt they didn't plan for her to get pregnant. She never wanted to be a mom. Lord knows why she even had the baby, but she did." I was waaa-yyyy too curious about Graham and almost leaned forward as Janet continued. "She passes through town once in a blue moon, just enough to make Allie wish she had a mother. Graham's as solid as they come. His hands are full between work and being a father."

"So, are there a lot of firefighters around here?" I asked.

I was still absorbing that detail about Graham, and my curiosity about him was a flame burning higher and higher. The man who was now my neighbor, and the man who'd laid the best kiss of my life on me when I thought I'd never see him again, of course he was a firefighter. That fit.

"We have a surplus of firefighters around here, hotshots and regular," Janet replied.

"What's the difference between a hotshot firefighter and a regular one? They're the ones who go out in the wilderness, right?"

Janet nodded. "Not much other than wilderness in most of Alaska. The crews around here are smoke jumpers. They fly out and land right in the middle of the fires. It sounds exciting, and I suppose it is, but it's not an easy job." Pausing, she dampened a towel under a faucet and wiped the counter as she continued talking. "Until this year, he was on the town crew, but he's the superintendent for a new hotshot crew here."

"How many crews are in town?"

"Willow Brook is thick with firefighters and hotshots, all of them too good looking for their own good. The Fire & Rescue station here serves as a hub for three hotshot crews and a town crew. Graham's a good neighbor to have. Make sure to get his phone number. If you ever need anything, he'll be happy to help."

I couldn't even imagine asking for Graham's phone number, but I bit back the urge to snort a laugh. At least he hadn't arrested me the other night. Even though he wasn't a cop, I didn't doubt if he'd truly thought I was breaking and entering, he'd have done his best to make sure I stayed put until the police arrived.

"I'll make sure to ask him," I commented as a bell jingled behind me, and I glanced toward the door to see some customers entering. "Thanks for the coffee." I turned back and cast a quick smile at Janet.

"Always. Hope to see you often. My sandwiches are pretty good too," she offered with a grin.

"I'll be back." I waved as I turned and left the café.

My budget didn't allow for having coffee out every day, but it was nice to meet Janet and get a feel for the town. Willow Brook was a far cry from Houston, but it was a cute town, and people seemed friendly.

I slipped into my car and quickly checked my notes on my phone. I needed some things at the grocery store. I'd stocked up on food yesterday, but I'd forgotten to get a few household items, such as toilet paper. There was one roll, but I needed more, along with some cleaning supplies. Although the house appeared to have been cleaned, it was still dusty.

My heart pinched thinking of my grandfather. I'd never gotten to see him as much as I'd wanted over the years. It didn't surprise me he didn't talk about his family with many people around here. He and my mother had a bitter relationship. He'd never liked my father. When my father tried to force my grandfather to invest in his business, he'd refused. After that, he and my mother hardly spoke.

I wondered if my grandfather had known more than I did about my father's business instincts. I shook my head to myself as I drove through town and turned into the parking area of the grocery store. I hurried through, scooping up everything I needed, and then headed home.

As soon as I realized I was starting to think of this place as "home" in my own thoughts, even though I'd only been here since yesterday, uncertainty stole through me.

The anxiety hovering inside me over the past year had become familiar. It was this cold unsteadiness inside, as if a door had been left open to a home and cold air was blowing through. I didn't like the feeling. I also didn't like that I was getting used to it.

As I drove toward home, I admired the view. I still couldn't quite believe I was living here. The mountains were tall in the distance, their hulking form both intimidating and comforting. They were so solidly *there*.

A few minutes later, I walked inside, and Wilbur greeted me enthusiastically with a few sharp barks as he circled my legs, his chunky bottom bumping into my calves. I kicked my boots off and quickly crossed over to the kitchen to unload the bags from the store onto the counter. I knelt to greet him.

"Hey, sweet boy," I murmured as I stroked my hands down his sides. He licked under my chin.

There was nothing like a dog's love, purely unconditional. Humans were much more complicated. If only I could get through life with a dog as my family. It would be so much simpler.

After I put everything away, I sat down on the couch to get up to speed on my email and follow up on a few feelers I'd put out for work. I tended to do my work at home on the couch because Wilbur preferred it. He liked to snuggle up beside me, and I found the background noise of the television soothing.

Today, I left it on a cooking show. Between emails, maybe I would learn something. Although this one was a rather cutthroat competitive show.

I squealed aloud as I scrolled through my email. I actually had a reply. I opened it with more excitement than I wished. I hated that I'd felt so comfortable in my position in my family's business, only to literally have all of it yanked out from under me. Confidence had never been my strong suit. I was learning I'd created some sort of façade by doing the things I thought I should do. Learning it was all wrong had dented my fledgling faith in myself.

Although my fingers itched to reply to the email instantly, I forced myself to type up a reply in a document and wait an hour or so before sending it. I didn't want to appear too eager. It was also a pet peeve of mine that people sometimes waited forever to reply to things.

I scratched Wilbur's neck, and he let out a satisfied rumble as he rested his chin on my knee. I idly watched the show. A man with a buzz cut who zoomed about the kitchen confidently appeared crushed when he lost a round in the cooking show. A matronly woman who had no professional cooking experience had wowed the judges with some kind of soufflé.

"See," I said to Wilbur. "She's succeeding on her own merits."

Wilbur blinked at me before closing his eyes. I leaned my head back against the couch with a sigh. That was the problem. I didn't even know what my own merits were anymore.

The only thing I felt confident about was my work. I couldn't exactly list my father as a reference, and I didn't want to. Fortunately, I had a few colleagues and people whose projects I had handled who were willing to serve as references and thought highly of my work.

I stood from the couch and strode into the kitchen, returning with a small plate with cheese and crackers on it. I was a sucker for good cheese and hoped my tight budget would get me through the next few months. If I played it carefully and started to find some work, it would be more than fine.

I'd paid for the year ahead on the internet. I figured that would force me to stay put, which I needed to do. Even if this place was brand new to me, I knew I needed to burrow in and try to find some stability.

I sat back down on the couch, kicking my feet up on the coffee table and taking a bite of cheese. After I finished chewing, I eyed the plate, commenting aloud, "Starving is worse than not having internet."

Wilbur lifted his head, wagging his little nub. "You just want the food." I slipped him a piece of cheese, which I knew I wasn't supposed to do, but he really liked cheese.

While I was watching the next challenge on the cooking show, which involved something to do with a maple glaze and a dessert and all seemed more complicated than I could handle, my phone rang. I eyed it suspiciously where it sat innocuously on the coffee table. I didn't get a lot of phone calls. Not lately. As I was reaching for it, I saw my former fiancé's name on the banner across the screen as it continued to vibrate in my palm.

"Asshole," I muttered.

Curiosity got the best of me, and I slid my thumb across the screen to answer.

"Hi, Dirk. I'm surprised to hear from you."

"Hi, Maddie."

It grated on me that he called me Maddie, and my mind flashed to Graham's daughter asking me if anyone called me that. The few who did were mostly people I'd known in high school and Dirk.

"What can I do for you?" My tone was crisp and sharp.

"I can't find my jet ski."

"Excuse me?"

"I can't find my jet ski," he repeated.

"Dirk, why the hell would I know where your jet ski is?"

"Because it was in our shared storage space. None of your stuff is there anymore."

I let out a groan. "Of course my stuff isn't there. It's not *our* shared storage space anymore. We had an entire email exchange about this, and you took over the rent and the paperwork. Also, since apparently you can't remember, you lent your jet ski to that friend of yours from San Antonio. I can't recall his name."

My ex was quiet for a moment, and I thought he was going to be an ass about it. He surprised me. "Ah, you're right. I totally forgot about that."

"Obviously."

"How are you?" he asked next.

"I'm well," I lied. "Yourself?" I countered politely, almost annoyed at my habit of asking friendly questions.

"I'm fine. Any updates on your father?"

"No, Dirk. It's not going to change. I'm not going to suddenly have money again, if that's what you're hoping for. How about we end on a friendly note? Call your friend, get your jet ski back, and carry on with your life."

"It isn't just about your money." Dirk sounded offended. "I can't deal with the complications of being associated with your father's business, and that includes you."

"Look," I began. I stopped. There was no sense in engaging in this back and forth with him. "Good luck, and take care."

After hanging up the phone, I felt that restless anxiety and unsteadiness inside that had become far too familiar over the past year. Standing, I crossed over to the windows and looked out into the darkness. Somehow the afternoon had slipped into evening without me noticing. It was so different here from Houston. For one, it was much colder, and it wasn't even winter yet. A half-moon was rising in the sky, its light gilding the tops of the evergreen trees in silver and casting a pearly glow on the mountain range in the distance.

I heard the thump of Wilbur jumping off the couch and his claws clicking on the floor as he trotted over and plopped down beside my feet. My dog was incredibly loyal, and he probably sensed I felt out of sorts. My heart squeezed, and I leaned over and trailed my fingertips between his ears. He smiled up at me.

"Wilbur, you're my best friend. Considering no one else has stuck around, I'm glad I have you." He blinked up at me, and my eyes stung with hot tears. I turned and crossed the living room, walking into the kitchen to fetch him a treat from a small bowl.

I was grateful that my grandfather had actually left dishes and kitchen items here. I hadn't even thought about that when I'd packed up my car and started the long drive from Texas to Alaska. My grandfather likely didn't know what a blessing it was he left me this place. When he died, my father's business was still in full swing, so he couldn't have known I would lose my job and most of my money within a few months after his death.

Wilbur snatched the treat from the air when I tossed it toward him. He hurried over to his dog bed in the living room just in case I might try to steal his treat from him, or something ridiculous like that.

My phone was still in my other hand when it vibrated again. When I glanced at the screen, it said "Mother." I'd kept it simple. I loved my mother, but we weren't on the best terms lately. Considering that I'd already had one annoying phone call with my ex, I figured I might as well get this one over with.

"Hello."

"Hi, Maddie," my mother began in her crisp tone. Although she was born and raised in Texas, her Southern accent was hardly there. She had the slightest hint of a twang and nothing more.

"Hi, Mom. What can I do for you?" As soon as I spoke, it occurred to me that I usually asked her that. I'd always tried to be helpful, to be the daughter who always had something to offer my parents. Which felt weird because now I knew unless I gave them what they wanted, it didn't matter.

"I'm wondering how you're doing there."

"I'm fine. The house is nice. Grandfather kept it updated."

"Of course he did. Your grandfather might have pretended he didn't care about money, but he could only do that because he always had plenty. He liked his creature comforts."

I bit the insides of my cheeks to keep from snapping back at her. "How are you?" I asked.

"I suppose as well as could be expected under the circumstances. Your father has a hearing next week, and I was wondering if you had reconsidered being more helpful to him than you've offered thus far," my mother said sharply.

"Mom, I can't. I'm not going to falsify any records. I had no idea what was going on, and obviously, I was an idiot."

"Maddie, you've lost your job and most of your savings. Don't you want that back?'

"No, not at the cost of this. I'd like to be able to keep my professional reputation intact. As it is, I'm not in a great position because of what Dad did. I respect that you want me to somehow fix this, but I can't do it by lying. I just won't. Please. I love you, and I'm sorry."

I hung up quickly because I knew how things tended to go with her. She would lay on the guilt thick. I hated this feeling more than anything. I hated learning that I'd been stupid. Everything that had given me confidence before turned out to be scaffolding made out of paper. Once it started to tear, everything fell.

Now, I didn't know how to believe in myself. A man I thought loved me didn't, or at least not unless I could deliver what he wanted—social connections and an entry into high society in Houston. I'd let down my father and my mother for refusing to manipulate the finances. Not that I knew how to fix it because I didn't even know what my father had done beyond the broad strokes. Apparently, I'd been running risk assessments on numbers that were falsified to begin with. The whole thing felt like a bad dream. Being so far away from it all made it seem even more like a dream. It was distant now.

I needed to make my own way without relying on my family. I felt like such a fraud, inside and out. Closing my eyes, I took a deep breath and tossed my phone on the coffee table. I might as well take a bath in that nice tub. Baths were free because the water came from a well. Yay for me! Of all the things I thought I'd ponder in life, my water and power sources hadn't been on the list.

A short while later, I looked at my feet where they rested on the curved edge of the bathtub. My toenails were painted a deep shade of purple. I'd wanted something to cheer me up, and I had plenty of nail polish. I laughed dryly with a touch of bitterness. For a woman who worried a lot about how she looked, I now lived somewhere where it didn't seem to matter all that much. The joke was definitely on me.

I rolled my head to the side and looked out the window from the tub. I could see lights glittering in the distance through the trees. I couldn't help but wonder if that was where Graham and his daughter lived. The moment I thought of him, I remembered our kiss. My skin was already flushed, but it felt like flames danced over the surface.

## Chapter Seven

# GRAHAM

"Do what?" I asked.

"Toss me that chainsaw."

"I'll *hand* you the chainsaw," I said dryly as I glanced over at Russell.

He rolled his eyes. "Fine. I didn't figure you'd be throwing the chainsaw."

I hefted the lightweight chainsaw and handed it over to him. We were working on clearing an empty lot and creating a giant pile of debris to burn. Planning ahead to manage fire-risk wilderness was part of being a hotshot firefighter. It was good for training and smart planning. Alaska was on the other side of decades of spruce bark beetle kill, which had wiped out swaths of the forests. We routinely cleared and had planned burns in areas to prevent fires from getting out of control.

We were still hiring for this crew and were up to ten so far. Today, I was out with Russell Dane. I'd known Russell for years. Like me, he'd grown up in Willow Brook. Unlike me, he hadn't stuck around after high school. But then, he hadn't been tied down with raising a daughter on his own. Not that I was complaining. I wouldn't trade having Allie for a foot-loose life for anything. I loved her so much it hurt sometimes.

Russell winked as he took the chainsaw and strode away, calling over his shoulder, "I'm going to take care of this tree over here."

I eyed the tree in question, a spindly and completely dead spruce tree. "Looks good. It's clear all around so you can just let it fall."

Leaning over, I fetched a water bottle off the ground and drained it as I watched him make quick work of the tree. It fell with a thump. I tossed the empty water bottle by my backpack and snagged a small ax and handsaw.

I set to work cutting off the small limbs on the fallen tree while he started the chainsaw again and cut up the lower portion of the trunk. We worked effi-ciently together. Once it was done, I asked, "You glad to be back in Willow Brook?"

"It's been almost a year."

I chuckled. "I know, but sometimes people come and go. You seem to be sticking around."

Russell nodded, and when my eyes slid sideways to his, I saw a flicker of something there. He'd had a rough patch after his father died in a firefighting acci-dent the very first month he'd returned to town.

"It's good to be home. It's kind of funny how much it's the same while also being different."

"What do you mean?"

He set the chainsaw on the ground and took his leather gloves off, swatting them on his battered work pants. "There are lots of the same people around, and it feels like home. But the town's getting a little bigger. We've got that new pizza place and that art gallery."

"Things stay the same and different everywhere in some ways, I suppose," I replied.

He eyed me for a long moment. "You ever wish you'd moved away?"

I shrugged. "Not really. It would have been nearly impossible to raise Allie without having my family nearby. I love it here too."

Russell nodded slowly. "You ever see Alison?" he asked, referring to Allie's mother.

I rolled my eyes. "Not much. Once in a while, she blows through town."

"Does she even know Allie?"

"Of course she does. I have full custody, though. I let her visit when she wants, but it's hard on Allie because it's never consistent. She'll sometimes go more than a year without seeing her."

He shook his head slowly. "That's bullshit, man."

I'd long ago come to terms with the situation with Allie's mother. I didn't want things to be different for me, but I wished they were for Allie.

"I shoulda known better. I thought she was hot, just didn't know how easy it was to get someone pregnant. My only excuse is we were young and stupid."

Russell's brows hitched up.

I shrugged. "It's pretty fucking easy when you're not using birth control."

He cocked his head to the side with a wry grin before his gaze sobered. "I gotta say, I never thought Alison was any deeper than a shallow puddle, but I didn't tag her as the type who would bolt right after she had the baby. I've got nothing but respect for you, man. Allie's one lucky kid to have you for a father."

"Having Allie turned out to be the best thing that ever happened to me. She's an amazing kid."

"I can't even imagine having a kid, and you've got a

fourteen-year-old daughter," he replied, his tone wondering.

I chuckled. "The years just keep on rolling along. I'm worried the next few are going to be the hardest. I thought it couldn't be harder than when she was a baby. But babies don't talk back and throw serious attitude, and you don't have to worry about guys."

Russell threw his head back with a laugh. "Good luck with that, man."

At that moment, Rowan Cole approached. He was a new hire and new to Willow Brook. He wasn't new to firefighting, though, and seemed like a solid guy so far. "What's so funny? Also, we got any water?"

"There're a few bottles over there." I thumbed over my shoulder to the small cluster of backpacks.

He crossed over as Russell replied, "Just laughing about Graham dealing with a teenage daughter."

"Good luck with that," Rowan said as he returned to us, water in hand. "I've got a teenage sister, and that's freaking stressful. The worry is endless, and I'm not even her dad."

I sighed. "Allie's a good kid. I'm just hoping she'll stay that way."

"Keep that shotgun close," Russell offered.

I cast him a glare. "I do, although she knows how to use it too."

Late that afternoon, I pulled up at my house and pocketed my keys, hoping Allie didn't have too much homework tonight. Lately, she'd been struggling with math and asking me for help. I'd freaking hated math in high school, but I was still trying. When I entered the house, it was quieter than usual. I peered in the kitchen, and there was no sign of her. She usually did her homework at the kitchen table.

I toed off my shoes and called out, "Hey, Allie-cat."

Walking down the hallway, I heard her respond, "Hey." Her voice was muffled through the door.

I showered when I got home from work because I was usually filthy, so I hustled into the bathroom. A few minutes later, I was walking back out and noticed her door was still closed, which wasn't the norm. When I came home, she usually came out of her room if she wasn't already. I knocked lightly on her door.

"Need any help with your homework?"

"No." Her voice sounded sniffly.

"Can I come in?" Just the possibility of my daughter crying had my heart twisting sharply in my chest.

"If you want."

Ah, hell. Something was up. When I opened the door, she was sitting cross-legged on her bed. Her elbows were resting on her knees, and she was staring down at the bedspread. Her cheeks were pink, and her eyes were puffy.

"Hey, what's wrong?" I crossed over quickly, sliding my hips on the bed.

She lifted her eyes to mine and knuckled at a tear that fell off her eyelashes. "Mom called."

I didn't swear, but I had to grit my teeth. I asked, "Oh?" Sometimes I thought I should get extra credit from the universe for my noncommittal replies to anything related to my daughter's mom.

My daughter's eyes looked just like they did every time her mom let her down—sad and tired and brave, all at once. "Remember how she said she was going to come visit soon?"

I nodded slowly. "Yeah."

Allie sniffled. "Well, she's not. She has a new boyfriend and a new job."

"I'm sorry, hon. I know you really wanted her to

visit." Those were words I'd said more than I'd *ever* wanted. Fuck this bullshit.

Allie sniffled again, swiping her hands over her cheeks and smearing her tears. I shifted closer, sliding my arm around her shoulders.

"It'll be okay," I said, my words feeling utterly inadequate. I'd gotten used to feeling inadequate when it came to parenting. That was the thing no one warned you about—constantly stumbling as you tried to get it right. Just when you thought you'd nailed something, your kid was another year older, and you had to figure out an entirely new obstacle course.

"I know." Her voice was muffled as she tucked her head against my shoulder. "I'm never going to have a mom to do my nails with, am I?"

"I don't know, hon. I can't make any promises on your mother's behalf." I'd said something to that effect hundreds of times.

"Can we have spaghetti for dinner?"

"You know it." That was one of the few things I could cook well.

"I'll help," Allie said, lifting her head and smiling a little.

My heart ached at seeing her puffy eyes. I couldn't help but smile back, though, because my daughter was spunky and resilient. These moments of upset about her mother usually passed quickly. When she climbed off her bed, I followed. She walked with me into the kitchen and began chattering about school as we pulled out the ingredients together.

## Chapter Eight

# GRAHAM

"Please," Allie said, the pleading look in her eyes not doing me any favors.

It was on the tip of my tongue to say no, but my daughter didn't give up easily. Before I could even reply, she pressed, "Maddie said I could. I just want to do something." She threw her hands up. "And she has a dog. You said he was really friendly too."

I silently swore. I had, in fact, told Allie Madison's dog, Wilbur, was friendly. He *was*. He was a happy smile incarnated in canine form.

"Fine. You can go. I need you to check with her before you startle her by showing up unannounced."

That earned me a hard eye roll. Allie slipped her phone out of her pocket, promptly pulling up a number and sending a text. "Can you give me her number? I'd like to have it in my phone if you're going over."

Okay, that was a completely reasonable request. But it was also a convenient excuse to get Madison's number.

My daughter's eyes swung up to mine. "She didn't

give me permission to give you her number," she offered pointedly.

I gave her a skeptical look. "Allie, you're my daughter and you're going over to someone's home. It's a standard expectation that I have the phone number. I'm not really worried about what Madison might think about that."

"Why do you call her Madison?" Allie asked when she handed me her phone.

I pulled up her contacts and texted Madison's number to myself. "That's how she originally introduced herself to me. I know she told you that some people call her Maddie, but until she tells me otherwise, I'll keep calling her Madison."

Allie blinked at me. "I'm sad Harold died, but I'm excited to have a new neighbor. He wasn't here that much anyway. Maybe she can paint nails with me."

I didn't completely get it, but Allie really wanted someone to paint her nails with her. I'd offered, but she didn't take me up on it except for once. She had already snatched her phone back from me and was skipping down the hallway, sliding on her socks halfway down to stop precisely in front of her door. She'd perfected that distance years ago. She wasn't looking my way, so she missed my reflexive scowl.

I wished I was surprised her mother had canceled another visit with her, but it was expected. I was more surprised when her mother stuck to a plan.

Talk about listening to the wrong head back when I was a senior in high school. Allie's mom was the homecoming queen, and all I'd wanted was her. I was no asshole, but my hormones led the way. It was hard to fathom a more abrupt reality check than Allie's mom getting pregnant the last month of our senior year. To this day, I still didn't know the whole truth.

I'd honestly wondered for years if she'd thought having a baby was a quick shortcut to tying me down.

But then, she'd skipped town. Babies were a lot of work. I'd lived that truth deeply. After Allie's first month in the world, I'd handled raising Allie with a lot of help from my parents. Thank God for them.

I'd worked at the grocery store job that I'd started in high school. I'd volunteered for the fire department on the side in high school, and that got me into training. I'd been on the town firefighter crew for years here. I hadn't had the time to do the training to become a hotshot firefighter until I got Allie to the other side of elementary school. She was now in her freshman year of high school, and I still didn't know how I felt about that.

She'd always loved sports. Every fall, she ran cross-country. In the winter, she played basketball, and then come spring, she played softball. It was busy. I was grateful because she didn't mind my new schedule not hewing so closely to her school schedule. My parents helped out when I was out in the backcountry fighting fires.

I had misgivings about Allie getting close to Madison, but then, I knew it would be weird if I tried to prevent it. Willow Brook was a small town, and Allie was accustomed to being friendly with the neighbors. So was I. We counted on each other. If I singled Madison out as someone she couldn't be friendly with, well, that would make her more curious than I cared to contemplate.

I couldn't exactly say to my daughter that I was hesitant because I wanted Madison for all the wrong reasons. Our kiss was tattooed into every cell of my body. The memory of the feel and scent of Madison conjured fiery jolts throughout my body.

"She said yes!" Allie called a minute later as she came skipping out of her room. "I'll go over after school."

"Okay. Sounds like a plan. You can call if you need anything when you're there."

"I'll text you, Dad," she said, her tone exasperated. She frequently reminded me of how slow I was on the uptake when it came to technology. She was not a fan of phone calls.

I was relieved she was in a cheerful mood. Last night had been tough after her mom called. She'd stopped crying, and we'd enjoyed dinner, but she'd been melancholy, and I knew it. She hated when her mom canceled, but sadly, she was accustomed to it. She was as realistic as one could be about one of their parents being mostly absent in her life. I knew it hurt, and I hated that my little girl had to carry that ache in her heart.

Not much later, I dropped her off at school and headed in to work. Willow Brook Fire & Rescue was in the midst of an addition. When I showed up, the sound of hammers pounding and some kind of pneumatic-powered tool filled the parking lot. I looked over to see Amelia Masters, Cade's wife, with a hammer in hand and a tool belt around her hips as she put some framing in place. It said something about what a good business Amelia and Lucy ran when there hadn't even been a rumbling about the town hiring them to do the addition for the station. With Cade being a superintendent here, his father the police chief, and Lucy's husband another hotshot firefighter, it was easy for people to complain about nepotism, but there hadn't been a peep.

I snorted to myself as I crossed the parking lot and glanced up to see Lucy working, her long blond ponytail blowing in a gust of wind. One of these days when I managed to save up a little extra money, I intended to hire them to do an addition on my house. Allie and I could use the extra space, and I might not mind a garage. It was sacrosanct to complain about the snow in Alaska. But it wasn't great in the long dark winters to wake up and shovel it off my truck. I also wanted to plan for when Allie started pestering me to drive.

I called over. "Hey, Amelia! Hey, Lucy!"

They waved back and carried on working. As soon as I stepped into the back hallway at the fire station, I encountered Levi with two cups of coffee in hand. He stopped at the door when I held it open. "Thanks, man."

"They're not gonna stop work to take a coffee break," I teased, glancing over my shoulder. I was proved right when Levi called Lucy's name, and she replied, "I'm busy."

I chuckled, and Levi rolled his eyes. "Here, you have one then."

He handed me a cup and followed me down the hallway. "What's on the radar for today?" I asked.

"You've got a couple of interviews lined up. Want me to stick around?"

"Sounds good to me. I hate hiring people unless I know them," I answered.

I'd been stoked to get the position as superintendent for the new crew, but it meant some work as far as hiring. Fortunately for me, there were a few local applicants, all people I knew. The rest were coming from outside the area. Hotshot firefighting was a coveted job for people who enjoyed the work, but it wasn't for the faint of heart. Firefighting was hard all on its own. Throw in flying out to the wilderness and dropping into fires from above with heavy equipment on your back, and it was next level. It was critical to have a well-trained and trusted crew. Everyone needed to be able to handle pressure, deal with the isolation, and not play games. The last thing any hotshot crew needed was tension amongst the crew. They ended up being like family.

"I'll take all the help I can get," I added. "I think I have five interviews lined up today."

"Rex said he's been sitting in on the ones you've done so far."

"He has. You know him; he likes to know who's coming into the station."

We stopped by the office space I shared with Cade, Beck, and Ward. Levi followed me into the office and plunked down in a chair at a round table in the corner.

"You think they're gonna have all that framing done before the snow flies?" I asked as I sat down across from him.

Levi nodded. "Oh, yeah. My girl runs a fast business with Amelia," he said as if I had somehow been questioning that.

I rolled my eyes as I dropped my backpack on the floor and took a seat across from him. "I know that, but it's just the two of them. Do they ever hire on extras?"

Levi ran a hand through his dark blond hair and shook his head. "They've tried a few times, but Lucy tells me they work well together and they'd rather do less work and do it the way they want. Most people who do construction are men, and they don't love having two women as their bosses."

I chuckled and took a swallow from the coffee. "Damn, that's good. This isn't from the office here."

"I picked up one of the coffee boxes at Firehouse

from Janet. I'd tell you to get some more, but I'm guessing it's already gone."

"Course it's gone. I feel lucky Lucy told you she was busy," I teased.

Levi gave me a lopsided grin. At that moment, Rex poked his head around the door, asking, "You guys ready?"

I waved him into the room. "Come on in." Spinning in my chair, I snagged the laptop on the desk and opened it, tapping the screen to life. "Our first interview is scheduled in ten minutes."

Rex came in, taking a seat at an angle from Levi. He held up his coffee cup. "I got some of that coffee. Who brought that over?"

I thumbed toward Levi, and Rex dipped his chin in acknowledgment. "Good move. It always makes for a more cheerful morning when we have good coffee."

"I didn't have time to stop there either. Allie was a little late getting ready for school, so we were cutting it close."

"She's growing up fast," Rex commented with a shake of his head.

"Don't I know it?" I replied with a sigh before taking a bracing swallow of the rich coffee.

"Life happens fast. I've already got a grandkid, and I can't believe that sometimes."

"Isn't Ella expecting?" Levi asked, referring to Rex's daughter.

"She is." Rex's eyes crinkled at the corners with his wide smile.

"How far along is she?" I asked because I hadn't caught up on this bit of news yet.

"Four months," Rex said.

"You ready for two grandkids?"

He nodded firmly. "It goes by in a blink. Sometimes, I miss when Georgia and I had young ones around the house. Being a grandparent is better than being a parent, though."

I placed my hand on my chest over my heart. "Man, don't start with that. I'm not even ready for Allie to have a boyfriend. I'm kind of hoping maybe she'll want to become a nun."

Levi burst out laughing just as Russell peered into the office, his brows hitching up as he looked around the table. "You still need me?" he asked.

"Of course, you're on the crew. I need your opinion. Is Beck still coming?" I glanced at Levi.

"I don't know. Let me ask Maisie." He leaned toward the desk and tapped the intercom button on the phone. "Hey, Maisie, where's Beck?"

"He's late getting in. He stopped to help fix Carrie Dodge's mailbox. Someone hit it with a car last night," she explained.

"Well, damn, that's not cool. Glad Beck is fixing it," I replied, along with the other sympathetic murmurs around the table.

"Hey, it isn't cool, but at least her cat wasn't involved," Maisie said.

We all knew Carrie. For one, she'd lived in Willow Brook her entire life and was now in her eighties. We also occasionally got called out to her place to rescue her cat, Herman, when he got stuck in a tree. The most famous incident was when she attempted to rescue him on her own with her late husband's excavator, and it fell over in a ditch. Thankfully, both she and the cat made it out unscathed.

"We'll start without him then," Rex said.

"You'd better," Maisie replied, "because your first appointment is already here."

We plowed through four interviews, and I wasn't

feeling great about any of them. I looked around the table, asking, "What do you think?"

Levi shook his head along with Rex. Russell ran a hand through his hair and nodded in agreement.

"We only have one more. Paisley Banks."

"Paisley?" Russell prompted.

I nodded. "Yup."

Levi tapped the intercom button. "Is Paisley here?"

Maisie replied promptly, "She's been waiting. Shall I send her back?"

"Please do."

A moment later, the sound of footsteps preceded the appearance of Paisley. The footsteps slowed, and we heard Maisie's voice. "Here we go. Don't let them try to intimidate you. I'm mostly in charge around here, so just keep that in mind," she explained, her tone dry.

Maisie grinned when she looked around the edge of the doorway. "Hey, guys."

I glanced over as she gestured to the woman beside her. "This is Paisley Banks."

Paisley had her auburn hair pulled back in a pony-tail that swung as she walked. Rex cast one of his smiles at her. He had the kind of smile that made anyone feel at ease. Paisley's green eyes bounced around the table. She looked a little tense until her gaze landed on Rex.

"Have a seat." Rex patted the chair beside him, scooting his chair over slightly as Paisley walked in.

We did a round of introductions. "So, you've got some good experience," I began.

Paisley nodded. "I think so. I trained as a hotshot firefighter in Washington, and I've worked in several states out West. I love the work."

"What brings you here?" Levi prompted.

"I always wanted to come to Alaska," she said simply. "As a hotshot firefighter, I'll get to see more of the area."

"Where there's fire," Russell interjected.

Paisley slid her eyes to him and nodded solemnly. "Well, that's the job."

I sensed tension from Russell. I liked Paisley. She was solid and steady, and she had a good feel to her.

We finished the interview, and once we heard the door close down the hallway, Rex said, "She's good. I think you should hire her."

Russell interjected, "I think she's going to be a distraction."

I eyed him. "Why?"

He shifted his shoulders. "You're not blind. She's beautiful."

"And?"

"I don't know," he muttered, looking disgruntled.

I gave him a considering look. "I've never known you to have an issue with women. There are several who work on the crews here. Is that a problem for you?"

He shook his head quickly. "I guess I didn't think about it much. This is a hard job."

"It is, and she's been doing it for five years. She obviously knows what she's facing. Her references are rock solid," Levi interjected.

With Levi in agreement, I headed up front to ask Maisie to start the official hiring process. There was a shit ton of administrative stuff associated with hiring, and I was profoundly grateful Maisie handled most of it.

After helping on a town call later that afternoon, I headed home. I'd temporarily forgotten Allie was over at Madison's place this afternoon until I got home and she wasn't there. I slipped my phone out to text Allie when I saw the text I'd sent to myself from her phone with Madison's number. I changed the contact from *Maddie Neighbor* to *Off-Limits Neighbor*. Maybe that would keep me sensible.

## Chapter Nine

# GRAHAM

It was getting late, and Allie still wasn't home. Snagging my phone off the kitchen counter, I sent her a quick text.

Me: *ETA? I thought you said you'd be home in time for dinner.*

I opened the refrigerator, sighing when I recalled I'd meant to swing by the grocery store on the way home today. It was one thing to forget to feed myself, but I had Allie to consider. Just then, my phone rang, and I lifted it to see my mother calling.

"Hey, Mom."

"Hi, Graham. I was wondering if you and Allie wanted to come over for dinner tomorrow night."

"Of course," I replied.

That was an easy yes. My mom was a fantastic cook, and I actually liked my parents. Maybe tonight, I'd just drive back to town to pick up a pizza.

"Excellent. How are things with you?"

"Busy, but what else is new?"

She laughs softly. "You're always busy. I heard

Alison canceled another trip. Did Allie know she was coming?"

"Unfortunately, yes," I said, leaning my hips against the counter and running a hand through my hair.

"How did she take it?"

"She cried, and then I made spaghetti."

"Smart man. You're a good father."

"I try. I forgot to go grocery shopping this week, though, so I'm zipping back into town to get some pizza for dinner."

"By the way, I heard you have a new neighbor."

I chuckled. "News travels fast. I'm glad Harold's house isn't going to sit vacant."

"I'm sure his granddaughter is nice."

"She seems nice enough," I said, keeping my tone nonchalant. My mother was the equivalent of a bloodhound following a scent when it came to picking up on things from me.

"Oh, have you met her?" my mother asked, her voice lilting. This was her nosy voice. I knew it well.

"You didn't hear the whole story? Rex called me because he got a report about somebody seeing the lights on there. Janet was the only one who knew his granddaughter was showing up, but she didn't know when. I ended up checking on the place. I don't think she loved me showing up like that, but she handled it. I didn't even know Harold had a granddaughter, but Allie did."

My mother laughed warmly. "Your daughter knows how to get the scoop, and Harold had a soft spot for her. Tell me about your new neighbor then."

"I just told you she seems nice."

"That's it?"

"Mom, I've met her three, I mean, two times. I don't know much more."

"Three times!" She practically barked in my ear.

"Two times," I corrected. I was lying, but I wasn't about to fill my mom in on my encounter with Madison before she landed in Willow Brook. "We ran into her at Firehouse Café too. Allie's over there now. I'm gonna have to check on her because she's running late."

"Well, be nice to Madison. It's not easy to move to a small town."

"Jesus, Mom. I'll be nice to her," I insisted, thinking in the back of my mind that my mother probably didn't equate being nice with kissing.

That kiss was a one-time deal, and I was blaming it on Madison. "I will absolutely be a good neighbor. We'll see you tomorrow night."

After getting off the phone, I pocketed my keys and jogged out to my truck, calling into Alpenglow Pizza to order two pizzas once I started driving. Allie still hadn't replied to my text. If she didn't reply soon, I'd stop by Madison's place on the way home.

In short order, I had pizzas in the truck and still hadn't heard a peep from my daughter. This wasn't like Allie. She was usually record fast with her replies because her phone was practically an extension of her body.

I didn't want to blame this on Madison, but I was disgruntled when I got to her house. I recognized Wilbur's sharp bark when I knocked on the door. I could hear Allie's laughter in the background. I had to knock a second time before I heard footsteps approaching.

Madison swung the door open, looking way too pretty. Her hair was pulled up in a messy knot with loose tendrils dangling around her cheeks and along the sides of her neck. Her cheeks were pink, and she was wearing sweatpants and a T-shirt. My eyes dipped down, taking in the way the shirt stretched across the generous curves of her breasts.

I yanked my gaze up when she said, "Well, hi there, Graham. Allie just checked her phone."

I nodded, almost not trusting myself to speak to her since my body felt too charged. "Allie," I called.

Allie came into the entryway looking relaxed and happy. She held up her hands and wiggled her fingers. "Look, we did our nails together. What do you think?"

Madison unsettled me, and I was annoyed that my daughter couldn't be bothered to check in with me. I didn't mean to be snappy, but I was. "I think you should've checked your phone and let me know you weren't going to be on time for dinner."

Allie set her chin in a mulish line. "It's not a big deal, Dad. My phone died, and I didn't have my charger. I didn't even think about it until just a few minutes ago."

"I let her use my charger as soon as she told me," Madison said, her tone placating as she glanced back and forth between us.

"It's fine," I said, probably too sharply. "You ready?"

My daughter looked like she wanted to cry, which frustrated me further because I didn't want any of this to happen in front of Madison. I was always working to be a halfway-decent father, and now I probably looked like an ass.

"You don't have to be so cranky about it," Allie said as she spun away. She would have stalked, except she was wearing socks, so it didn't have much impact.

Wilbur circled my feet excitedly, and I finally leaned down to greet him. Madison's tone was low when she spoke. "I'm sorry. I wasn't paying attention to the time. You could have texted me."

"It's fine," I replied.

Allie had been an easy kid for most of her child-hood. In the past year or so, I felt like I was fumbling and screwing up over and over. I didn't know how to deal with her having an attitude, and her emotions could shift in a blink. Her doctor told me hormones were the reason, but that didn't make me feel any better when I didn't handle things well.

A moment later, Allie returned, shrugging into her jacket and stuffing her feet into her boots. She looked toward Madison. "Thank you. It was nice to visit. I'm sorry my dad's a jerk."

"Allie," I began.

She slid me a look, and I stopped. As it was, I didn't even know what else I meant to say.

"Good night," I managed.

As we left, Allie paused to stroke Wilbur's head, and then we were gone. I felt Madison's eyes boring into my back as we walked down her stairs and crossed the drive to my truck.

Allie gave me the silent treatment on the way home. I decided that was better than the alternative, which was an argument. When we pulled up in front of our house, I said, "I have pizza for dinner."

"I thought you were going to the grocery store."

"I forgot."

"Oh, sort of like how I forgot to charge my phone and didn't pay attention to the time. So, it's okay for you to forget, but not me?"

I turned to face her. "Allie, I don't ask much. You could have checked the time and just sent me a text. No biggie. I'm sure Madison would've let you use her phone."

Allie pressed her lips in a line. "Next time, I won't

forget. I'm glad you got pizza, but we don't have any oatmeal or yogurt for breakfast."

She flounced out of the car. After we ate, the tension settled. I apologized for being cranky, and she apologized for forgetting to let me know when she'd be home.

The following morning, it was Saturday, and I didn't have to work. Allie was sleeping in. Even though every fiber of my being protested it, I knew I needed to apologize to Madison for being cranky in front of her. After a cup of coffee, I sent Allie a text, letting her know I'd be back shortly. I figured I wasn't required to notify her that I was going to apologize to Madison. A subtle tension spun inside me that I wasn't telling her where I was going, but I would go to the grocery store after that. Technically, I wasn't lying completely.

I was in the kitchen after a shower, wearing my robe and looking forward to some fresh coffee. Wilbur let out a bark, and I heard tires on gravel. I had no idea who would be showing up on a Saturday morning. I only hoped it wasn't another neighbor wondering who I was. I walked from the kitchen toward the entryway, peering toward the door only to see Graham standing in the window. He lifted his hand in a wave.

I darted back quickly. Fuck. Graham unsettled me every time I saw him. My traitorous hormones went wild whenever he was nearby, even last night when he'd been all grumpy.

Answering the door in a robe wouldn't be the end of the world, but still. Wilbur looked at me curiously. He was excited to see Graham and ran to the door, his little butt wiggling like crazy.

"I don't exactly have a choice," I said to myself in the hallway. "He already knows I'm here."

I tightened the belt on my robe as if somehow that would protect me. After a deep breath, which did next to nothing to slow my rampaging pulse or quell the heat swirling through my body, I walked into the entryway. My eyes landed on my bare feet, reminding me of Allie's request to paint her nails. She'd been so excited about it. She'd also mentioned her mom had canceled a visit, and it broke my heart a little bit. I'd stumbled into that conversation without any context. She'd shown up with nail polish. What was a girl to do? I couldn't say no.

Lifting my eyes from my feet, I opened the door, and my pulse took off like a horse out of a gate at the sight of Graham. His brown curls were damp, and his deep blues landed on mine. My belly did several spinning flips, and my skin felt hot and prickly all over.

"Hi," I said, my voice coming out all breathy.

"Morning." He dipped his chin in acknowledgment.

Wilbur was ecstatic, letting out little yips as he circled Graham's ankles. I bet even his ankles were sexy, and I'd never paid attention to anyone's ankles.

Graham knelt to pet Wilbur, and my ovaries swooned. "Morning, Wilbur," he said in that low gravelly voice he had. "He sure knows how to make someone feel welcome."

He straightened, and his eyes landed on mine again. As soon as our gazes made contact, it felt like a sizzle sparked through the air. I cleared my throat. "He does. It's always good to see him at the end of a long day. He thinks I'm the best person ever."

Graham chuckled, and that sent a prickle down my spine while my belly shimmied and swooped. "I wasn't expecting you here this morning," I said inanely.

Wilbur barked and started to dash off the porch. Graham's reflexes were lightning fast as he leaned down and scooped Wilbur into his arms. We looked out to see something dart into the trees.

"What was that?" I asked.

"I think it was a coyote. I just saw the tail, but that's my guess. Can I come in?"

Wilbur was wiggling like crazy in his arms, but Graham had a good hold on him. "Of course."

I stepped back, opening the door wider as he walked through. He didn't release Wilbur until I closed the door firmly. Wilbur gave him an affronted look once his paws were on the floor before scurrying to look out one of the windows that flanked the door.

"Do I have to worry about coyotes too?" I asked when I looked up at Graham.

He nodded. "It's Alaska. There are plenty of coyotes around, and you might see the occasional wolf, although those aren't as frequent. It's fall, so the coyotes are pretty well fed. If you're around next spring, you'll definitely want to be careful because they're looking for easy food. Do you let him out much on his own?" He nudged his chin toward Wilbur.

I shook my head. "He only goes out when I go out. I don't usually keep him on a lead because he's a good boy, but I should probably be careful."

"Definitely."

"Would you like some coffee?" I heard myself asking.

*What are you doing offering him coffee?* my brain screeched. *That means he's going to be here long enough to have coffee, and our hormones can't handle that.*

My hormones were all, *Hell yeah, we can! We can take a nice long look at Graham.*

Graham looked surprised, but he nodded. "I always say yes to coffee."

He followed me into the kitchen. "Have you been in here before?" I asked.

"Not many times, but yes. Harold spent about

six months of every year here. He wasn't huge on having visitors, but I would stop by and check on him."

Graham's gaze whisked around the space. "Looks the same. Janet took good care of it for you."

"She did. I'm grateful he had someone checking on the place."

I crossed over to the counter, fetching a mug from the cabinet and filling it with coffee. "Cream or sugar?" I asked.

"Neither."

I gestured to the table by the windows. "Have a seat." I did have manners. I wasn't going to kick him out now that I'd offered coffee. He sat down and took a swallow of coffee. His eyes lit up. "Good, you like it strong."

"I don't see any point to coffee that isn't strong."

Wilbur had lost interest in the front door and entered the kitchen, plopping down beside my feet when I sat down across from Graham. "So, what brings you here this morning?"

He took a swallow of his coffee, and my eyes lingered on the motion of his throat. I blinked, trying to focus. Sweet hell. I even thought his throat was sexy.

Oblivious to my state, Graham commented, "I'm still getting used to having a teenager. Allie can get annoyed with me real fast."

"Most teenagers can," I offered gently. It was downright endearing to see the sheer worry in his eyes about his daughter.

Graham shifted his shoulders, looking slightly uncomfortable. An uncomfortable Graham didn't dim the brightness of his hotness wattage. "Look," he began before pausing to clear his throat and take another swallow of coffee. "I was rude last night, and I apologize."

"You don't need to apologize to me," I said, shaking my head.

"But I do," he insisted. "Allie frequently loses track of her charger. Sometimes, I think her phone is actually an extension of her body, but the charger isn't."

I couldn't help the laughter that slipped out. "She *is* a teenager."

Graham rolled his eyes. "That she is, and it isn't easy sometimes."

"Like I said, no need to apologize to me, but thank you. I can't imagine trying to raise a teenager on my own. Talk about difficult."

My heart squeezed a little for him. This tough guy firefighter looked so uncertain. It was downright endearing to see him apologizing for being a grump. "Yeah. Kids don't come with an instruction manual. I figured that out when she was a baby. Unlike other things, every phase needs a new manual."

"She's a great kid. Obviously, you're doing a good job." He looked uncomfortable again and lifted a hand to run it through his rumpled curls.

My hormones got even more excited. I was on the verge of handing over my ovaries.

"She *is* a great kid. Here's hoping she doesn't hate me by the time she hits eighteen."

"She won't," I said confidently.

He shrugged. "She hates limits, and I'm not cool, and I can't paint her nails with her."

"Well, you *could*," I teased.

"I did let her paint my toenails once, but she said it wasn't the same as doing it with a mom."

"She's kind of a girly girl, and you're not a girly guy," I offered softly.

"I'd let her paint 'em again if she wanted, but she wants a mom."

"Oh."

There wasn't much more to say to that. I had so many questions, but I didn't feel like I knew Graham well enough to pummel him with my nosiness about why Allie's mom wasn't around. Her dad was all Allie mentioned, and she thought he hung the moon. Until he came over and gave her a little hell for not bothering to text him.

"Just so you know, if you'd rather her not stop over, all you have to do is say so."

"That's not how I feel. It would break her heart if I said she couldn't. She's a social kid. She used to like to come over and visit with Harold."

"How about we agree that when she does come by, I'll text you to confirm what time you can expect her back? I'm pretty good at keeping an eye on the clock, and I never let my phone die."

He nodded slowly. The sound of his rough chuckle sent goose bumps chasing over my skin. This Graham —whew. He was going to make me crazy. I was busy trying to tell my hormones to chill out, and they were blowing me off.

"Thanks for the coffee," he said a few minutes later as he stood.

Of course, it was only when I stood from the table that I realized I was still wearing a bathrobe. Gah! I was practically naked, and I'd forgotten about it. He followed me over to the sink.

"Shall I wash my mug?" he asked.

I looked askance at him. "No, I don't make company wash their own dishes."

His fingers brushed mine when he handed over the mug. It felt like fire sizzling over my skin. My belly flipped, and my pulse raced. I knew my cheeks were hot, and I prayed it wasn't too obvious. Unfortunately, that was a futile hope.

I turned to say something after I rinsed his mug and discovered he was still right there. The feel of his lips fitting over mine flashed through me. The memory was like a loud clap of thunder on the heels of lightning.

When I met his eyes, my breath caught in my throat. His gaze was intense. He lifted one of his big hands, passing his knuckles lightly over my cheekbone.

"You're dangerous, Madison," he murmured.

I'd never known a man's voice could get to me, but sweet hell, Graham's voice did crazy things to my insides. It felt as if my entire body was tingling. Need tightened in a coil in my center as I looked up at him. I tried to catch my breath, tried to say something sensible, but not a single word came out. A ragged sigh slipped out. It might have passed for a whimper if I had enough nerve to fess up.

"I knew it was a mistake to kiss you before," he whispered in that gravelly voice.

Insecurity reared its ugly head inside, and I opened my mouth to protest, but he placed his finger over my lips.

"Why?" I whispered when he lifted his finger a second later.

"Because I knew I'd want to kiss you again."

"I didn't think I'd ever see you after that," I murmured.

"Yet here we are."

My brain cells had all but immolated at this point. I felt myself leaning up to meet his lips because I needed another kiss from him more than I needed my next breath. The moment his lips made contact with mine, it felt like the lick of a flame. The heat spun into my veins, spreading fire through my body in its wake. He made a low, almost growly sound in his throat.

I went for it again. Because, dear God, this man made me feel desperate and needy.

## Chapter Eleven

# GRAHAM

I forgot all the reasons I shouldn't be kissing Madison. Every single one of them. They were like slips of paper tossed into a bonfire, the flames flickering high in the air. Everything about her was another piece of kindling tossed on the fire.

She was wearing a robe, for God's sake. How was I supposed to resist that? The moment she'd opened the door, I'd known she had just gotten out of the shower. Her cheeks had been flushed, her skin dewy, and her hair damp.

If it hadn't been for that stupid coyote and her dog about to chase after it, I'd have been able to keep my senses and never crossed that threshold. Yet here we were.

Her lips were plump and soft, and oh-so-*very* kissable. The way she arched against me with her body coming flush with mine drove me wild. She made these little sounds in her throat, spurs in the flanks of my need, sharp and driving, heightening the pace of it until there was no slowing it down.

I dove into the warm sweetness of her mouth.

Holy hell could she kiss. She wasn't shy, her tongue glided against mine in sensual strokes while her hand curled around the back of my neck. I could feel her fingers sifting through the ends of my curls. Everywhere we touched, which was a lot of places, it felt like lightning striking me. I was tight with need, the sheer electricity of it sizzling to the point of burn.

All I wanted was *more*. My hand slid down her back, and I finally cupped her sweet bottom. Her body was warm and inviting. That loose robe was nothing but a tease, showing off hints of what was hiding behind it. She let out another sound into our kiss, and I broke free, nipping at her earlobe. I loved the way she shivered against me before I let my tongue tease over the side of her neck. She tasted sweet and fresh.

I couldn't help it. I was feeling greedy, and I squeezed her bottom, gratified when her hips rocked against my arousal. Fuck. I was so hard for her I might as well have a tire iron in my pants. I let my hand slide away from the unholy temptation of her bottom and slid it up over the dip of her waist. I couldn't resist more. Her robe was calling for it—the way it fell to a V just above her breasts. Her collarbone was delicious, and the perfect place to tease kisses.

I trailed my fingertips along the edge of her robe, savoring when she let out a ragged gasp. "Graham, please."

I was pretty sure she needed what I needed, and I let my hand slide under that soft fabric to discover the lush weight of her breast. Her nipple was taut, and I teased the peak even tighter, loving how she trembled in my arms. As established, I wasn't thinking. So, I pushed the fabric out of the way and leaned down to catch that sweet pink nipple in my mouth. Her fingers speared my hair, and she gasped, crying out sharply when I drew a lazy circle with my tongue before giving her nipple a sharp suck.

I was riding the edge of insanity at this point. The only thing that stopped me was Wilbur. I heard the sound of claws skittering across the hardwood floor, followed by a sharp bark. We broke apart abruptly, staring at each other.

We were breathing raggedly. And, fuck me, she was a sight to behold. Her hair had started to dry in waves around her shoulders. With her robe open and one breast exposed, she looked wanton. Her nipple was pink and damp from my attention, and her skin was flushed with passion all over. It was all I could do not to reach out and push her robe off her shoulders so I could see everything. But then, I knew I'd be taking her on the counter. Kissing her was beyond dangerous. My need for her ran roughshod over any sensibility I had.

Wilbur barked again, and Madison finally tore her eyes from mine, quickly pulling her robe into place and tightening the belt. She started to move, but I caught her lightly by the elbow.

"It's probably a bird or maybe that coyote," I offered.

She stared at me with kiss-bitten lips. I wanted to kiss her again and lose myself in the fiery heat that burned between us. I opened my mouth to speak, but she shook her head quickly. "Please don't apologize."

I stared into her eyes, surprised to see a swirl of uncertainty there. I didn't know what that was about, but I felt compelled to say, "I wasn't going to apologize. I'm not sensible around you."

Madison blinked, her cheeks flushing a deeper shade of pink. It was so endearing I wanted to kiss her all over again. In all honesty, my need to kiss her hadn't diminished one tiny bit.

"It seems I'm not sensible around you either," she whispered.

Wilbur barked again. This time, I followed Madison out front. We peered through the windows flanking her front door to see a raven perched on the top step of the porch and eyeing Wilbur with a touch of arrogance. At the sound of another bark, the raven gave him one last look before hopping down the stairs and flying into the trees.

I fumbled through a goodbye. I didn't even know what I said, and then I found myself on the porch while she looked at me from the doorway. "Have a good day," I finally said.

I didn't even know what she said in return because the need rushing through me was roaring so loudly that I had to force my feet to keep moving, or I was going to kiss her all over again. I didn't think I'd be able to stop this time.

As I drove away, I was beyond annoyed with myself. I couldn't be starting some kind of crazy fling with my sexy neighbor. The list of reasons that was a bad idea was endlessly long. Although she didn't look like her, something about Madison reminded me of Allie's mother. I'd be willing to bet money she was homecoming queen in high school. She had that vibe. If not that exactly, she'd definitely been the kind of girl my not-so-smart-head would've wanted when I was young. Hell, I wanted her now. Fiercely.

I shook those thoughts away, reminding myself I needed to think about my daughter. Actually, I knew what I needed to do—go to the grocery store. I was almost relieved to have a task, anything to distract me.

## Chapter Twelve

# GRAHAM

The following weekend, I walked past the living room, studiously ignoring the giggling escaping into the kitchen, and sat down at the table. Allie was having friends over tonight. Overnights were the bane of my existence. It felt like teenage hormones descended upon the house.

I glanced around. There were empty pizza boxes on the counter. Blessedly, the girls had cleaned up and already put their dishes in the dishwasher. If I'd learned one thing as a parent, it was making sure to mention the good stuff. I reversed course and leaned into the living room.

"Thanks for cleaning up your dishes, girls," I called over the cacophony of voices.

It was amazing to me that only three of them could make so much noise. They turned to look at me from where they sat on the floor in front of the couch. "You're welcome. Thanks for noticing, Dad," Allie called in return.

"Can we have ice cream?" her friend Serena asked.

"Of course. I picked up three flavors at the grocery store."

I was feeling a little too proud about that detail. The next thing I knew, the kitchen, which I thought of as my safe space during slumber parties, had been taken over.

"Ooh, raspberry chocolate chip. My favorite!" Allie dashed over and pecked a kiss on my cheek.

"There's also regular chocolate chip and that peanut butter stuff," I offered.

It only took another few minutes, and they returned to the living room with their ice cream. I put some in a bowl for myself and sat at the table, contemplating making a cup of coffee. I didn't really need one, but coffee was always good. That said, the girls were probably going to keep me up as it was.

Of course, thinking of coffee had me thinking of Madison. Madison who made a mean cup of coffee. Madison who I'd seen at Firehouse Café again this morning. Madison whose kiss I'd replayed *waaa-yyyyy* too many times in my thoughts. Just thinking about it now caused me to shift in my chair.

*You can't pursue her. There's nothing there. You don't have time. She's complicated. And she's way too prissy.*

*You don't know that she's prissy.*

My less critical thoughts intervened. I *didn't* know that. She just *seemed* prissy with her glossy dark hair and her perfect mouth. She was always put together. Even her robe was nice. But she couldn't be *that* prissy since she'd driven up to Alaska by herself.

I had so many questions about Madison, and I wanted to know every answer. Why did she show up to live in her grandfather's house? This small town in Alaska was a world away from a city like Houston, Texas.

I gave my head a hard shake, telling myself I needed to stop thinking about Madison. I knew it was probably futile. She was my closest neighbor now. This town was too small for me to avoid her. Not to mention, she'd painted her nails with my daughter. I didn't want to be rude to Madison, but avoiding her wasn't polite. There was no way I could get around it in Willow Brook.

The girls eventually quieted down, and I retreated to my bedroom. They decided to lay in sleeping bags in the living room because they wanted to fall asleep in front of the fireplace.

The following morning, I was in the kitchen getting coffee after Allie's friends had left. I heard what I thought was the distinct sound of my daughter crying. It was weird how attuned I was to that sound. She was in her bedroom with the door closed, but the subtle sniffles were magnified to my ears. I set down my coffee cup and walked quietly down the hallway, hoping she didn't hear the sound of my socks on the hardwood floor.

Yep. She was definitely crying. I was debating whether to knock lightly on the door when she called. "Come on in, Dad."

So much for my stealth moves. I opened the door slowly, peering around it. "Sorry. Need anything?"

Allie looked up from where she sat in the center of her bed with her legs crossed and her elbows resting on her knees, her usual crying position.

My heart squeezed. "What is it?" I crossed to her bed and sat on the end.

"I called Mom."

A jolt of anger struck me, but I kept my face passive.

"I wanted to know when she was going to visit again since she canceled this one."

"Ah." I nodded slowly. "What did she say?"

Allie's head dipped down. She pressed the heels of her palms in her eyes, smearing the tears away. She didn't look up when her hands fell to her lap. "She doesn't know."

"Ah," I repeated, the neutral response I used when I didn't know what the hell to say. "I'm sorry, hon," I finally added. "Do you want me to talk to her?"

My daughter's eyes lifted, and my heart twisted painfully in my chest. They were red-rimmed, and her lashes were spiky from her tears. For a second, I saw hope flare in her eyes, and then her shoulders curled down as she let out a ragged sigh. "No, there's no point, but thanks. What are you doing today?"

"Not working. Want to go to Anchorage? We can get lunch at your favorite place."

Allie shook her head, her curls swinging. "Can we go to Firehouse?"

"Of course." As if I'd say no to anything she asked just now. Good thing what she asked for was an easy one.

Later that afternoon, while Allie was ensconced in her bedroom watching something on YouTube, I decided to call her mother anyway. Alison answered on the fourth ring.

"Hey, Graham. What's up?"

Her tone was dry, and annoyance pricked at me. "I'm not calling to ask you to visit Allie, but I would appreciate it if you didn't make promises you never plan to keep."

"Jesus, Graham. No need to be so high and mighty. I'm in a new relationship. When things settle, I'll try to take a look at my schedule."

"Because that's going to change something," I returned swiftly. "Look, I have done my damnedest not to be an asshole, but this has got to stop. I want her to have a relationship with you, but please stop making promises. You're ruining any chance you have for her not to think you don't care."

Alison sounded chastised when she replied, "Okay. I'm sorry, Graham. I didn't mean to hurt her."

"You never mean to hurt her, but you haven't been a parent so you don't know what it's like."

"I'm a parent!" she retorted defensively.

"Being a parent isn't just having the baby. You were here for the first month of her life, and then you bolted. Since then, you've visited, what? Maybe six times. You're a parent insofar as your name is on her birth certificate, but that's it. If you keep doing this, I *will* go to court and pull visits."

"You would never—" she began.

"Yeah, I would. You don't visit as it is. Your own parents would testify against you at this point. I've never asked for child support, and I'm not about to. All I'm asking is you don't make our daughter promises you don't intend to keep. That's it. I gotta go."

I hung up because there simply wasn't anything else to say. I fucking hated this situation. I loved being a dad, and Allie was a part of my heart. But filling the hole her mother left in her life was a constant battle. Alison was a flake—shallow and superficial—and just couldn't be bothered.

I laughed to myself, the sound bitter to my own ears. She'd seemed like a great girl in high school— gorgeous, fun, and the life of any party—but not a good option to raise kids. I'd been a little startled she'd even decided to have Allie. Maybe she was too far along when she found out, and her parents pressured her. She'd never said much about it to me.

I took a breath, willing the anger to pass inside. Just then, my phone vibrated, and I looked down, seeing *Off-Limits Neighbor* flash on the screen.

Off-Limits Neighbor: *What do I do about a moose between me and my car?*

## Chapter Thirteen

# MADISON

Graham: *Be right there.*

I was seriously relieved when Graham replied right away. I peered out my window again, eyeing the large creature. Unlike the time I'd seen the moose at the gas station, this one was closer. I'd seen a few others since I arrived in Willow Brook. They were plentiful in Alaska. So far, they'd all been at a distance.

This moose was easily taller than my car. It had long gangly legs and a giant head. Wilbur was quiet after his initial bark and just stared curiously through the window. I wondered how long it would take Graham to get here.

Only minutes after I'd sent my text, I heard the sound of approaching tires on the gravel. A moment later, Graham's truck appeared. The moose turned and looked toward his truck. Graham drove right up to it and laid on his horn, causing the moose to meander off at a lazy trot. After a few minutes, he climbed out of his truck.

I watched as he put a shotgun in a small compart-ment behind the seats. I held Wilbur's collar as I opened the door a moment later. "Why did you have a gun?" I said by way of greeting.

"Because if the horn didn't chase him away, I would've fired the gun. Don't worry, I wasn't going to shoot the moose."

He stepped through the door as I gestured him in and closed it quickly, locking it for good measure. "How often will I see moose?" I demanded.

"Maybe every other day sometimes," Graham replied with a chuckle as I looked up at him.

"Seriously?"

He nodded slowly, and my belly did a quick somersault. Jesus. This man was too hot for my sanity. His hair was rumpled, and he looked a little tired. He also smelled woodsy, and I wanted to kiss him all over again.

I swallowed, ordering my traitorous hormones to get a freaking grip. "Thank you for coming over so fast."

"No problem."

Graham eyed me for a long moment as we stood there. Wilbur started sniffing around his feet, and Graham knelt briefly to greet him before straightening. "I should get home. Text if you need anything."

After he left, I wondered how I was going to keep my sanity with a neighbor like him.

———

A week had passed since I'd sent out emails and completed some online job applications. When I opened my email to find one from an energy company in Anchorage, I let out a little squeal. They wanted me to contact them for a preliminary phone interview.

Wilbur came running over, bouncing up and down by my feet.

"Wilbur, I have a chance to get a job. This is great news!"

I chuckled to myself. After being something of a workaholic for years, I'd been feeling restless. I needed to work, and I wanted to feel useful. My savings was only going to last me for so long. "I think this means coffee," I said to Wilbur.

He wagged his entire body in response. After taking a shower, I drove into town, my eyes landing on Willow Brook Fire & Rescue as I drove by. I wondered if Graham was at work. My forays into town had demonstrated several things. Everyone knew everyone here, and nobody hesitated to be nosy without me even introducing myself. People seemed to know that I lived in my grandfather's old place. More than one person had commented on Graham being my neighbor and further that he was a firefighter, a nice guy, and a single father.

I could see the questions swirling in people's eyes about me. I was curious about my new town and uncomfortably inquisitive about Graham. Since he'd hurried over to chase off that moose, I hadn't seen him. Allie had stopped by for a visit again. As agreed, I'd texted him. She was a sweet kid. I didn't need any reminders that Graham was a good man, but his daughter was also one of them letting me know how great her dad was.

A few minutes later, Janet was smiling at me. "What can I get you today?"

"I'll take your mint chocolate latte. I'm kind of in love with those," I replied with a sheepish smile.

"Well, they're delicious."

After she prepped my coffee, she opened a drawer

under the counter and handed me a card. "This is for Jasmine. She's an artist at the gallery. Ethan and Jack own several galleries here and in Seattle. They're really nice people and are looking for an accountant. You do that, right?"

I looked over at Janet, and tears almost sprung to my eyes as emotion crested high inside. This woman, who'd only known me for weeks at this point, actually cared. "I do that. Thank you. I didn't expect this." While I was technically an actuary and dug deep into financials and other information to assess risk, I was also a skilled accountant. After what I'd just gone through by putting all of my eggs in one basket, I was thrilled to keep my options open.

Janet's eyes were warm. "You're welcome. I had a soft spot for your grandfather, and I know he loved you. We take care of each other around here."

"I can see that," I said slowly.

Just then, another customer arrived at the counter. "Thanks again."

I stepped away, taking a sip of my mint chocolate latte. The sweet flavor slid over my tongue, and I let out a happy sigh as I crossed over to sit at a table. I looked out over Main Street, smiling at the sight of the tiny town. I was starting to think maybe I could make my new life work.

When I was back at home later that afternoon, I was surprised when my phone vibrated with a text. Not many people sent me texts. When I saw Graham's name flash on the screen, I was even more surprised. I tapped to open it.

Graham: *I need a favor. Can you pick Allie up at the high school? I'm out on a fire call, and I forgot to ask my mom to pick her up. My mom's at a doctor's appointment so she can't go get her.*

Me: *Of course! Can you tell me where the high school is?*

Graham: *At the end of Main Street. Just follow the signs. I'll be out of cell range for a while. Should be home in a few hours. Thanks.*

Me: *No problem, I'll pick her up.*

"Wilbur, I'm going to get Allie. Do you want to come?"

Wilbur wagged as he looked up at me. He trotted by my side after I tossed on a jacket and grabbed my purse. I quickly texted Allie to let her know I was on my way. She replied almost instantaneously.

Allie: *I know.*

Once I got to Main Street, I drove past the cluster of shops before I saw the promised sign for Willow Brook High School. A few minutes later, I was waiting in a line of cars. I chuckled to myself. This was the kind of thing many parents complained about—the drop-off and pickup at school. It was a novelty for me, though, so I didn't mind.

Wilbur was excited, pressing his nose against the passenger seat window as he looked outside. It was a full five minutes as we inched ahead in line. Once we got close to the front of the school, I scanned the area to find Allie. A moment later, I saw her lifting her hand and waving. She adjusted her backpack on her shoulders and started jogging toward the car.

"Wilbur. Get in the back." I patted the seat, and he turned, hopping onto the console and jumping into the back seat.

Allie slipped her backpack off her shoulders quickly as she slid into the front seat. "Hi."

Wilbur leaned forward and licked her cheek when she turned to greet him. "He's very excited to see you," I commented.

Allie stroked his face. "Do you take him every-where you go?" she asked.

I shook my head. "I don't like to leave him in the car. Should I take you straight home?"

Her eyes took on a gleam. "Can we go to Firehouse?"

"Is that okay with your dad?"

"I'll text him."

"Don't text him. He's out on a call," I said quickly. "I'm sure it's fine. You're not allowed to have coffee, though."

Allie let out a put-upon sigh, but when I glanced sideways, I could tell she was amused. "I'm allowed to have chai tea or hot chocolate."

"I might have to get one of those hot chocolates with you. I saw the specials menu for those the other day."

"The mint chocolate is the best."

Allie scrunched her nose. "Actually, it's a tie between that one and the caramel. So good."

A few minutes later, we were on the way to Main Street. "How was school?" I asked.

"Fine. I'm a freshman, so I'm on the bottom of the social totem pole," Allie offered matter-of-factly.

I laughed softly. "Oh, high school. It can be rough."

"I bet it wasn't rough for you."

I glanced her way as I slowed at a stop sign. "What do you mean?"

"You're pretty, and you always look put together. I'm not so great at that."

I shook my head as I turned. "That's not true." Allie had brown curls paired with her big blue eyes. She was a lovely girl.

Allie sighed. "It is. I don't know how to style my hair, and I don't know how to do makeup."

I recalled that I'd wanted to wear makeup at her age. My mother hadn't allowed me to wear any until my junior year in high school.

I didn't even know if that made sense, and I didn't know what the rules were about this kind of thing. "You don't need makeup," I countered, and I meant it. Allie was adorable.

"Of course you're gonna say that. Dad hates talking about looks, and my grandparents tell me I'm the best thing ever. Everybody's trying to make up for my mom not being here. She's beautiful. She was the homecoming queen in high school."

"She was?"

I slowed, turning on my blinker as we approached Firehouse Café. I glanced sideways quickly to see Allie's ponytail bouncing as she nodded. "She was. I've seen her pictures. She was beautiful. She still is."

"Where does your mom live now?" I couldn't help asking.

"Not here."

I parked and looked toward her. Allie was staring out the window. Even though I couldn't see her face, I knew she was upset. "My mom's parents live here, but I'm not as close to them as I am to my other grandparents. They're awesome." She turned to look at me, and the pain I saw in her eyes hit me like a punch in the chest. "My mom left when I was only a month old, and I've seen her—" She held up her hands and started counting with her fingers, stopping at the ninth. "Nine times. She always says she's going to visit every year, but she doesn't. She just canceled a visit last week. Dad felt bad, and that's probably why he let me go over and see you. He feels bad and sad because I'm kind of a girly girl. He's kind of a guy-ly guy." Her mouth twisted, and the sadness faded. She laughed softly. "If you know what I mean."

"Guy-ly guy. I like that. He definitely is pretty guy-ly," I offered.

Allie giggled and moved to climb out of the car. I wasn't thinking when I reached over and placed a hand on her shoulder. "I'm sorry about your mom," I said quietly.

She turned back, her eyes holding mine for a long moment. "Thanks. I can't complain. I have an awesome dad, even if he gets on my nerves some-times." Her lips curled into a smile, and I squeezed her shoulder.

We climbed out of the car together and started walking into the café. "It's obvious he loves you. Didn't you tell me he let you paint his toenails once?"

Allie burst out laughing as we walked into the café, the little bell giving a cheery welcome when we crossed the threshold. We approached the counter and waited in line. This place was starting to feel comforting to me. I didn't know that many people in town, but everyone was always friendly here, and it was warm and cozy. A cool gust of air blew in as another group of customers entered.

A moment later, we were at the front of the line, and Janet smiled between us. "Hi, ladies. What can I get you?"

"I'm going for the caramel hot chocolate," I offered before glancing at Allie. "What about you?"

She scrunched her nose. "Mint hot chocolate."

"Where's your dad?" Janet asked as she began getting our drinks ready.

"He's out on a call, and Gram had a doctor's appointment, so Dad asked Maddie to pick me up. Isn't it awesome that she's our neighbor?"

Janet handed Allie her drink, smiling at us again. "Of course, and she's lucky to have you and your dad as neighbors."

"I still miss Harold," Allie said hurriedly. She glanced at me.

"I do too, and I'm glad to have y'all as neighbors. It's nice."

"Why do you say y'all?" she asked after taking a sip of her hot chocolate.

I shrugged. "It's a Southern expression, an abbreviation of you all."

"I like it. It's gender-neutral, so I'm going to start saying it, but I don't think I can do it with your accent."

Janet chuckled as she handed over my caramel hot chocolate. I paid for both of our drinks and mouthed, "Thank you," as Janet began waiting on the next customers.

Allie stopped to greet a couple, a tall man and a small petite woman with blond hair, as we were walking out. "Hey, Jasmine," she said. "Nice to see you, Donovan. Maybe I can come work on some pottery with you next week?" Her voice lilted with a question when she looked back at the woman.

"Anytime," Jasmine said. "Like I told you, Saturdays are when I'm doing cleanup. It's a good time for you to stop by."

The woman's eyes landed on me curiously, and Allie gestured to me. "This is Maddie. She lives in Harold's old place. She's his granddaughter and our new neighbor."

Jasmine smiled. "Nice to meet you."

"You too," I said, feeling a little shy.

The man with her glanced at me, dipping his chin. "Welcome to Willow Brook."

"Thanks."

Jasmine glanced at Donovan before looking back at me. "You know Graham then. He works with Donovan."

"Oh, you're a firefighter too?" I asked.

Donovan nodded. "Sure am. I'm off this week, but I hear Graham's crew is out dealing with a fire at one of those abandoned cabins a few hours north of here."

"Is that where they are?" Allie asked.

"According to the scanner," he replied.

Jasmine gave him a dry look. "Even when he's off, he likes to know what's going on and has to listen to the scanner."

Allie giggled. "We have one too. Dad does the same thing when he's off."

"Nice to meet you," Jasmine repeated as Janet called out a greeting to them.

"You too. I'm sure I'll see you around town," I replied.

Unlike Houston, that was highly likely. I was discovering that while I might be a city girl, I could get used to the cozy social world of this small town.

## Chapter Fourteen

# MADISON

Not much later, I was on autopilot and had turned down my own driveway. It was only when I stopped that Allie asked, "Can we go over to my house?"

Glancing sideways, I said, "Oh! I wasn't thinking."

She shrugged. "I want my nail polish so we can do our nails together. Let's just walk through the trees. I promise it's only a few minutes."

"Um..." I began because I hadn't considered this.

"I need to refresh my nails. You can pick a new color too," she offered.

"I don't want to leave Wilbur alone for too long."

"Oh, you can bring him inside. I promise it'll be fine."

"Are you sure that won't be a problem for your dad?"

Allie's brows hitched up as she rolled her eyes. "It'll be fine. Come on."

The next thing I knew, I was walking with Allie through the trees along a path while Wilbur trotted beside us, sniffing madly. I hadn't even taken the time to explore the woods around my new home. I was still adjusting to the fact that this was *my* home. I also wasn't particularly comfortable tromping around the woods by myself. I knew from the paperwork on the property that I'd inherited over thirty acres.

The distance from my house to theirs through the trees, as the crow flew, was roughly a ten-minute walk. It gave me comfort to know that I wasn't completely alone out here. I scanned the area once we reached the edge of their driveway. The home was a single-story ranch set amidst a cluster of trees. Off to the side was a view of the mountains in the distance.

"Pretty," I commented.

I stepped onto the porch that ran the length of the house and looked around curiously as we entered. The door in the center led to a small entryway. Through an archway were a living room and kitchen area with a small hallway off to one side, but that was it. I presumed that led to their bedrooms. The space felt masculine. It was decorated in charcoal gray and beige tones with a few splashes of color.

"I'll be right back." Allie kicked her shoes off, and I followed suit.

She gestured me toward the kitchen table. I crossed over to sit down as Wilbur began investigating the house. "Should I put him on a lead?" I called just before she began walking down the hallway.

She glanced back, shaking her head. "He can look around." She smiled down at him before looking back up at me. "I've been trying to persuade Dad to get a dog for a while. Our dog Banana passed away a while ago."

"Oh, I'm sorry!" I pressed my palm to my chest.

"Me too. Dad says he's too busy for us to get a puppy right now, but I'm working on him. Be right back," she repeated.

I looked around while I waited, sipping the delicious caramel hot chocolate. The combination of flavors was decadent. A few minutes later, Allie returned, setting down colors for me to choose for my nails. She also brought a bag of cotton balls and nail polish remover. I opted for a bolder shade—a rich plum—while Allie alternated bright blue with pearly white.

"What do you think?" She held her hands up and wiggled her fingers a little while later.

"They look great!"

I was starting to feel antsy, but not because I felt like I was doing anything wrong. I enjoyed spending time with Allie, but Graham had only asked me to pick her up because he didn't have any other option.

I knew our last explosive kiss was something he regretted. I didn't know how I knew he regretted it, but I just did. I also knew he didn't think we should be involved. Not that I was looking to be involved, but my confidence was so banged up. Sensing his hesitance about me only added to the uncertainty I felt about myself.

Long story short, I wasn't sure how wise it was to spend much time here with Allie. Before I could sort out what to do, Wilbur let out a bark when the front door opened. A moment later, I heard Graham's low voice as he greeted Wilbur and prayed that he wasn't upset that Allie had invited me in, along with my dog. He stepped through the archway from the entrance and looked over toward us.

My belly swooped at the sight of him. His dark curls were mussed, and he had a smear of dirt on his cheek. He was clearly in his work clothes, and he was so sexy, it took my breath away. Apparently, I had a thing for men looking roughed up and dirty. Or maybe I just had a thing for Graham.

His arms swung as he crossed over to us. "Allie invited me in. She said it was okay for Wilbur to come in," I said quickly.

He grinned as he looked over at her. "I figured. Wilbur's no problem. Thanks for picking her up. Where's your car?"

"I wasn't thinking and automatically drove to my place. Allie wanted to paint our nails." I held up my hand. "She showed me the path here."

Graham nodded. "I need to take a shower because I'm filthy, but I can drop you off after that."

"Don't forget I have a slumber party tonight," Allie called as he angled toward the hallway.

He glanced over his shoulder. "Right. Okay, I'll drop you off after I take Madison home."

"Dad, you promised we could go to Wildlands for an early dinner before you drop me off." She paused, her eyes bouncing from her dad to me and back again. "Can Maddie come with us? Please."

## Chapter Fifteen

# GRAHAM

It was obvious Madison was trying to stay out of this. She was inspecting her nails carefully and then began closing the bottles of nail polish. She also stood and put the empty hot chocolate cups in the trash.

I couldn't say no to Allie's pleading look. It was just dinner with my daughter and our neighbor. That's all it was. *Riiii-ght.*

I chuckled silently, my own mind taunting me. I wanted *a lot* more than dinner with Madison. I'd barely been able to shove thoughts of our last encounter out of my brain. Every single free minute I had, I remembered the lush weight of her breast in my palm and the way her nipple tightened to a peak. Her flushed skin and her passion-hazed eyes were vivid in my memory.

"We need to see if Madison can go," I finally said, forcefully kicking those inappropriate thoughts to the curb.

"Madison can go." Allie spun to her. "Come with us, please."

I bit back a laugh. Back when Allie was little and we'd practiced the manners song, I hadn't counted on her using her manners to sweet-talk me and others into what she wanted.

Madison's eyes shifted from Allie to me. When I saw the question swirling in hers, I nodded. It was fine for Allie to invite her, and I could keep my hands to myself. She looked back to Allie. "Sure. That'd be nice. I need to drop Wilbur off first, though."

"We can drop him off on the way," I said, my voice coming out gruffer than I intended. "Give me five to shower."

I hurried to the bathroom, tossing my work clothes in the hamper. Moments later, the water sluiced over my body, and I rolled my head side to side, savoring the hot water beating down. It had been a long afternoon. A branch had fallen on me when we were dealing with a fire at an abandoned cabin. The wilderness of Alaska was dotted with hunting cabins, some used with frequency and others forgotten and left in disrepair. Inexperienced hunters or hikers were prone to accidentally starting fires, which was exactly what had happened today. Fortunately, the cabin in question was tiny, and there weren't too many dead trees around it. We'd gotten it taken care of within a few hours. We were getting into autumn, and fire season was just now starting to slow.

I couldn't keep Madison out of my thoughts. I'd texted her in a pinch because my brain couldn't think of anybody else to ask to pick Allie up. Of course, after I texted her, I'd been able to think of a few other friends I could have called. It was a reflection of how deeply she'd burrowed her way into my thoughts. She was waiting in the wings and whisked her way into my consciousness.

I didn't need to be thinking about Madison when my teenage daughter was sitting in the kitchen with her. "Fuck," I muttered to myself. I finished showering and toweled off before tugging on clean jeans and a T-shirt. When I strode into the kitchen, Allie glanced up.

"That was seven minutes, Dad," she said, her lips pursed.

I chuckled. "Sorry. You ready to roll?"

Her ponytail bounced as she nodded. "Let me go grab my backpack. I already have it packed."

After she hurried down the hallway, Madison stood from the kitchen table, brushing her palms over her jeans. She looked up at me just as she smoothed a hand over her hair. Her dark locks fell in a glossy tousle over her shoulders. I wanted to wrap my hand around her hair and pull her close and kiss her. Now *that* was crazy thinking.

She cleared her throat just as I said, "Thank you for picking Allie up. I'm sure she appreciated you coming over to paint nails with her too."

Madison's lips twitched with a smile. "No problem. I did suggest she teach you how to paint your nails."

I rolled my eyes. "I'm a pretty good sport about it."

Madison's throaty chuckle sent electricity sizzling up my spine. Allie reappeared at the end of the hallway. "I'm ready."

In short order, we were in my truck with Allie in the middle of the bench seat practically vibrating with excitement. I sensed that Allie had decided to play matchmaker with Madison and me. Her instincts were spot-on because I did want Madison, but it wasn't practical, not at all.

While my body might want Madison, I knew she couldn't be right for me. We were nothing alike. She was always tidy and perfectly put together, even in the middle of the wilderness in Alaska alone on the side of the road when her dog was chasing a moose. I couldn't imagine her tromping around through the woods, much less really wanting a guy like me. I didn't dress up very often. When pressed, I could, but I always felt like I was wearing someone else's skin. The last time I'd worn a suit was at a friend's wedding. I'd spent the day feeling itchy and out of place.

I forced my mind to the moment and dutifully drove over to Madison's place. She hopped out. "I'll be right back." She hurried into the house with Wilbur excitedly following her. He paused by the steps to pee on a bush before bounding up the stairs.

Allie giggled. "What's so funny?" I asked.

"Wilbur's so cute."

I chuckled. He was currently wiggling at high speed as Madison opened the door. "He is a cute dog," I agreed. I waited for her to beg me to get a dog.

Instead, she said, "Thanks for letting us have dinner with Madison. It's nice. She's new."

I knew that feeling. I'd grown up in this very same small town. The lure of one new person showing up was exciting when you were younger. As an adult, I appreciated the town differently. I had plenty of friends and family for support. I loved where I lived. I didn't know how Allie would feel when she was older. If I hadn't had her, I probably would've wanted to leave and go to college somewhere out of town. She was young enough yet that she didn't bring it up often, but she loved meeting new people. I'd always assumed that was why she and Harold had gotten close. He was only here about half the year, and she loved it because he was a breath of fresh air.

"Everyone has to have dinner at Wildlands at some point," I commented.

Madison returned to the truck, and off we went to

Wildlands. All the while, I wondered just how big this mistake was. After I dropped my daughter off for her slumber party with her friends, I would be alone with Madison in the truck. I needed to think long and hard about what that might mean. Specifically, I probably needed to keep my hands to myself.

## Chapter Sixteen

# MADISON

I looked around the large timber-frame-style building with wide plank hardwood floors and exposed beams. The restaurant was on one end of the hotel with windows looking out over the lake. The setting sun cast a watercolor of pinks and lavenders over the water's surface. The bar ran the length of one wall, and tables and booths occupied the rest of the space. The place suited Alaska. Living in Alaska, it felt as if I was toeing the edge of the wild.

Allie wanted me to try the caribou burger with fries, so I did. After we ordered, Allie chattered about school, occasionally catching her ponytail in her fingers and twirling it in circles. I couldn't help the tension humming in my body. It seemed impossible to be near Graham without that electricity crackling to life. Ever since our last kiss went a little crazy, I kept reminding myself Graham wasn't good for me. He wouldn't want a girl like me, and I didn't need to be trying to have a fling, much less a relationship.

I was terrible at being casual. That was probably how I ended up getting engaged so young. I mentally chastised myself. While other girls managed to test the waters of dating in college, I couldn't seem to pull it off. I'd wanted so badly to please anyone, to be wanted. That was the downside to my distant parents, who mostly paid attention to what I could do for them.

I'd been ignoring another message from my mother, pleading with me yet again to talk to our father's attorney and "update" the paperwork. I swatted those thoughts away and looked around while Allie showed her father her grades on her cell phone.

"Well, hello," a voice said.

I glanced up to see an older couple approaching the table. I knew without knowing that these had to be Graham's parents. The man looked like an older version of Graham with his brown curls liberally salted with silver and the same intense blue eyes. The woman had silver hair twisted into an elegant knot. They stopped by the table, and Allie smiled up at them.

"Hey, Gram and Grandpa." She spun in her chair to stand and hug them both quickly. She smiled over at me. "This is Maddie. She's living in Harold's old place. She's his granddaughter."

"Oh, hello," the woman said. "I'm Rose." She held her hand out, and I stood to shake it. "This is my husband, Bill."

Graham's father smiled and reached out to shake my hand after Rose released it. "Nice to meet you. How are you settling into Willow Brook?"

I followed Allie's lead and sat down after she did. "I'm settling in, and I like it so far."

"What brings you here?" Rose asked next.

I wasn't about to share the truth—that my father was facing fraud charges, the family business was falling apart, and I'd lost my job in the aftermath—so I simply said, "When I inherited my grandfather's place, I took it as a chance to come see what he loved so much about the area. He meant a lot to me."

All of that *was* true, but I still felt as if I misled them. If things hadn't blown up in my father's business, I doubted I would ever have come here.

Graham's mother looked at me curiously and then turned her attention to Graham. "Heard you handled that fire this afternoon."

Graham dipped his chin. He was leaning back in his chair and had an elbow hooked over the side. He seemed oblivious to my unsettled state. "It's my job, Mom."

She smiled before her eyes shifted to me again. "Well, it was nice to meet you, Madison." She glanced at Allie while Graham's father said something to him. "I thought you had a sleepover tonight?"

Allie's chin bobbed up and down. "I do."

Now, his mother's look got even more curious when she glanced at me. I was certain she deduced that meant Graham would be driving me home. I felt like chiming in to explain we were just having a neighborly dinner, whatever that was. I held my silence, simply smiled and hoped my expression was calm and entirely unreadable. I didn't want Graham's mother to sense I was lusting desperately after her son, which was completely inappropriate because he had a daughter who did *not* need him having a fling with some woman he wanted nothing to do with. I hadn't forgotten Graham's initial reaction to me, and I knew he thought I was foolish.

After Graham's parents left, I breathed a silent sigh of relief. They were nice, really nice. Unfortunately, being around nice families elicited a prickle of unease. I didn't feel comfortable in my skin because I didn't know how to be around families like that. My legs were crossed, and one of my feet bounced restlessly. I willed it to stop. I couldn't do anything about the family I had. The past was one thing you couldn't change. I had the parents I had, and I didn't have a warm, friendly family. I told myself I was reading too much into it, but I hadn't missed the glint of wondering in Rose's eyes. I'm sure she thought I was totally wrong for her son, and I was. He was a good, solid man. It just so happened he was also ridiculously sexy.

Allie got up to go to the bathroom before we left, leaving Graham and me alone at the table. When I looked over and met his eyes, it literally felt as if a current of electricity snapped in the air between us. My pulse took off at a fast gallop, pounding through my body, while my belly did a little shimmy when his eyes held mine for too many beats of my heart.

"Your parents are nice," I blurted out.

He nodded, one corner on his mouth curling up and sending my belly into a swoop. I felt hot all over.

"They are," he said, his voice all gravelly and sexy.

"Do you like having them nearby?"

"Of course. I couldn't have raised Allie without them. Sometimes being in a small town can feel..." He paused and then shrugged. "Small. Everyone knows everyone. I'm sure you can guess that's why people are so curious about you. We get plenty of tourists in the summer, but it's major news when someone moves here."

Allie returned then. "Are we ready to go?" she chirped, bouncing on her toes lightly, her impatience showing.

"She's ready to go," Graham observed as he glanced at me with a wry smile. "You ready?"

I knew he didn't mean anything sexual in that comment, nothing at all. But my hormones were all, *Hell to the yes! We are ready.*

I simply nodded because I wasn't so far gone I couldn't manage to be polite. We stood, and Graham snagged the check the waitress had left on the table. He flipped his wallet out and promptly dropped several bills on the table.

I started to open my purse, and his voice stopped me. "I'm paying."

"You didn't expect to take me out to dinner," I protested.

Allie slipped her hand through my elbow. "Dad gets all manly about things like this. Just let him pay. You can get him dinner another time."

Feeling even more flustered now, I closed my purse with my free hand as I looked back and forth between them. "Thank you. I'll get our next meal."

Graham said something under his breath, but I didn't catch it. With Allie avidly watching us, I wasn't going to press the issue. We walked out to his truck together. Not much later, we had dropped Allie off for her slumber party, and Graham was driving back toward my place. The tension was practically killing me. I was tied up in knots inside, and my need was pulsing in electric waves through my body.

I managed to take a shallow breath, and asked, "What did you say when we were leaving?"

He stopped at a stop sign, and his gaze turned toward me. I'd swear lightning crackled in the space between us.

"You're not going to buy me dinner," he said flatly, his eyes daring me to argue.

I let out a puff of breath as he turned onto the

road. The sound of his blinker clicked loudly until he completed the turn.

"That's ridiculous," I replied. "We're well past the era where only men can pay for dinner."

"So what?" he scoffed.

"You are ridiculous," I muttered. I crossed my arms, tapping my foot on the floor.

His chuckle sent a wash of heat through me. Everything Graham did turned me on. He annoyed the hell out of me, and somehow even *that* turned me on. I could give the silent treatment like a pro, though. I stared out the window at the moon rising above the mountains and casting them with a pearly glow against the inky dark sky.

A few minutes later, the sound of gravel underneath his truck tires was all I could hear over the pounding of my heart. When he stopped at the end of my driveway, I turned to look at him. The engine quieted when he pressed the button to turn it off. With the sharp edge of desire riding me, I practically jumped out of the truck. By the time I rounded the front, he had climbed out.

We stared at each other, and I swallowed before saying, "Thank you—"

His words crossed over mine. "Thank you—"

I finished, "For dinner."

"For picking Allie up from school."

The air felt loaded and heavy. The distance between us felt malleable—massive like a chasm but also small and crowded. I could hardly catch my breath. All I could think was I needed to kiss Graham again.

I had no idea what he was thinking. His eyes were dark as he stared at me. In a flash, he caught my elbow in his hand and tugged me closer before I could even wrap my brain around what was happening.

"Madison," he murmured roughly. "I need to kiss you."

I couldn't even form a word, yet I was in complete agreement. Kissing Graham, right this very second, was a requirement of the universe.

His lips met mine, and it felt like a lightning strike where our lips met. Searing energy flashed through my body and set all of my cells aflame.

## Chapter Seventeen

# GRAHAM

None of this was graceful. I plastered Madison against my truck, caging her between my palms. The cool metal of my truck did nothing to quench the fire of need blazing through my body. Her mouth was warm and soft, her lips—sensual, plump, and cushiony—made for mine. All the while, her kiss was hot, slick, and overwhelming.

Our tongues dueled. There was no finesse, it was all a fiery mess. Madison made these little sounds in her throat that drove me fucking crazy. We broke apart, each of us gulping in air. It was chilly out tonight, enough that our breath misted in the air around us.

The only thing that snapped through the madness was the sound of Wilbur's sharp bark muffled by the door. She stared at me, her eyes hazed with passion. "I need to let Wilbur out."

Fuck me. Even that comment sounded sexy in her throaty voice.

"Should I go?" I heard myself asking.

I didn't want to go. I wanted to spend the night

with her and steal every minute I could have with her for myself. I usually had to think about my daughter, but she wasn't here. This felt like a stolen moment, something I could have.

I knew it wouldn't be more. Maybe it was stupid, but we'd already done stupid. We'd already snapped the ties of sanity by kissing more than once. I waited as the moment spun out between us, my heartbeat thundering.

Madison blinked when Wilbur barked again. "Do you want to go?"

I loved that she challenged me with that question. She was not a woman who would be vague about anything. Everything about her got to me, even when she was annoying.

"No, I don't," I finally said. "I want to stay. I want to make you forget everything except my name."

Her eyes widened slightly, and her nostrils flared as she took a deep breath.

"Okay. Well, come on in then," she whispered.

I stepped back from the truck and curled my hand around hers as we walked up to the house. She opened the door. Wilbur was beside himself, dancing around our feet as we both greeted him.

"Give him a second. He needs to do his business," she said.

I walked with her and Wilbur as we made our way down the driveway in the darkness. He stayed close and stopped to pee on a few trees. I chuckled when he paused to do his "other business" as Madison said.

"He looks like a canine comma," I observed.

She threw her head back with a throaty laugh that tightened the coil of need inside me. "He does. He's so short his body just curls a little."

Wilbur glanced our way. "It's okay, Wilbur," she

offered. "Humans aren't dignified either when we go to the bathroom."

Madison was a puzzle to me. I had tagged her as a prissy woman, more worried about her appearance than much else. I still wasn't sure how to categorize her, but I knew there was much more to her than the surface. I also knew I'd underestimated her and wasn't sure I liked what that said about me.

A few minutes later, we were in the house. Following her lead, I hung my jacket by the door and left my shoes next to hers. Wilbur had promptly curled up on his bed in the living room.

Madison lifted her eyes to mine. She took a breath, almost as if she were steeling herself. The sound of her swallow was loud in the kitchen. "You, um—" she began.

I reached for her hand, giving it a light tug, gratified when she closed the distance between us immediately. Then she was right there. Her presence was a force field vibrating near me. Need had its claws in me, and they were buried deep. I wasn't going to shake it loose until I had her.

"Let's make some ground rules," I murmured.

"Ground rules?" Her voice lilted.

"Yes. We're neighbors. As far as I can tell, you're going to be here for a while. I really want you. I figure there's no sense in denying that. But, as you know, I'm a single father. Dating, at all, is complicated. Let's stay friends, but that's it."

Madison blinked up at me and nodded. "I think that's smart. Do friends do what we're about to do?"

"These friends do," I murmured as I stepped closer.

Her body came flush against mine, and I could feel

the tight points of her nipples pressing through my T-shirt.

"So, tell me, is Wilbur going to interrupt us?"

Her breath came out in a short, sharp pant, and her lips curled in a rueful smile. "Probably, but we can let him sleep out here."

"Lead the way then."

She turned away, her hand curling around mine more tightly. She led me down the short hallway to a part of the house I'd never seen. As we stepped through the doorway, my eyes took in the bedroom—a tall ceiling with beams above and a large bed against the wall with a dresser opposite. There was a door off to the side, which I presumed was a bathroom.

Madison turned, and she suddenly looked bashful. The uncertainty flickering in her eyes was like a silken thread tossed and spun around my heart, cinching tightly. *This* girl—the one who had so boldly kissed me when she thought she would never see me again. This girl whose eyes were heated with passion looked unsure. It affected me in a way I was unprepared for. I wanted to wipe that uncertainty away.

I didn't allow myself to contemplate my reaction. I didn't want to. That would complicate things. I stepped closer, palming her cheek as I dipped my head to kiss her again. I knew I would lose all ability to think the moment her tongue glided against mine and was proven right instantly.

Kissing Madison was like standing in the midst of an electrical storm, the air itself sizzling from the power of the combined forces. She felt so fucking good. The soft give of her lips was pure pleasure, and the sensual tangle of her tongue sent fiery jolts spinning through me. And again, those little sounds she made—the hitch in her throat, the whimper as my palm slid around to cup her nape and then down her back in a smooth pass, smoothing over the lush curve of her bottom and pulling her against me.

My arousal was intense. I might as well have had a fucking bat in my pants. She gasped, and her hips arched into the cradle of mine. This was going to be fast and messy. But then, it seemed everything was with her. Definitely messy and too fiery hot to slow down. Contact with her was like a match at the end of the fuse with the flame racing toward its source.

Madison broke away abruptly, gulping in air. Seeing as I needed some myself, I took a ragged breath as we stared at each other.

"This is crazy," she murmured.

"It is," I agreed. "Crazy or not, we might as well burn this fire to ashes, then maybe we can be sane."

Her eyes went wide as she let out a soft laugh. "I suppose so." That uncertainty that I'd seen before flickered in her eyes. "I don't really do this."

"Do what?"

She gestured back and forth between us. "This. I've never had a fling. I had one boyfriend, and we got engaged."

For some reason, this shocked me. My shock must've been written on my face because her lips curled in a self-deprecating smile. She shrugged lightly. "It's true. I'm not really a casual kind of girl."

Once again, everything I thought about Madison was shaken and realigned. I'd imagined her like Allie's mom—shallow and flighty and stringing along guys in high school and college.

"Well, I'm your guy then because I'm not in the habit of flings."

She rolled her eyes. "I was saying that to warn you."

I stepped closer. "To warn me?"

She nodded and swallowed. "I don't know if I'm that good in bed."

"Huh?" I was flabbergasted.

Although the lighting was dim in her bedroom, I knew her cheeks flushed a deeper shade of pink. She shrugged. "I'm just saying I don't know if I'm good in bed."

"Sweetheart, I've kissed you. I'm not worried," I said flatly.

Suddenly, I had something to prove—not about myself but about her. I caught the hem of my T-shirt in my hand, dragging it up and over my head before tossing it to the floor. Her eyes widened, and she stepped back a little, her thighs bumping into the end of the bed.

"Oh!"

"Oh, what?"

Madison gestured toward my chest, her hand swiping up and down in the air. "Just you. You're in really good shape," she murmured.

"Well, yeah, I have to be. My job isn't exactly easy. Now, let's get to work."

"Work?"

"Oh, you're not getting to work, I am. It's the best kind of work," I clarified.

Madison simply stared at me. I closed the distance between us once again, this time catching the hem of her T-shirt in my hand and dragging it up over her head. I was gratified by her startled gasp and the way her mouth fell open in a pretty little O.

Of course, I should've known my knees might almost give out. Madison in a bra. Fuck me. She was to die for. I could see the taut peaks of her nipples, a hint of pink peeking through the black lace.

I didn't even wait a second before dipping my head and catching one nipple with my mouth. I sucked through the lace and savored her sharp cry as her fingers speared in my hair. I lifted my head and devoured her mouth. Because I needed her. Everything about her was like another sharp spur in the flanks of my desire. I was spun tight by the driving force. I didn't even want to hold back.

Our kiss got messy fast, and she stumbled a little, but that worked for me. I lifted her, sliding her hips onto the bed before pausing and straightening. "Wait a sec. You need more clothes off," I said matter-of-factly.

Madison's eyes were dazed as she blinked up at me. "Okay," she rasped.

She quickly got with the program. She slipped off the bed, unbuttoned her jeans, and shimmied out of them in a hot second. To torture me, she had silk panties to match her bra and her almost-black gorgeous hair. She hooked her thumbs over the edge of them, but I shook my head.

"Not now, sweetheart." She reached for the buttons on my jeans, and I shook my head again.

She lifted her chin, her eyes narrowing. "No fair, I want to see more."

"Oh, you will, but I need something to keep me in check," I said flatly.

And then, we were kissing again, stretching out on her bed, and Madison was pure fire. Her skin was silky against me, and she kissed with abandon. Once she stopped thinking, she threw herself into it. She nipped my lip, arching and flexing under my touch as I let my palms map her sweet body. Her belly trembled under my touch, her thighs shifting restlessly as I slid a palm down one. I found my way back up and cupped her mound, letting out a groan in her mouth when I discovered the wet silk there. I wanted to rush. I was near frantic to have all of her.

But I was going to make sure this was good. I didn't get nights like this. I didn't let myself have them. Madison was a person out of my world. Even though she was my neighbor, she wasn't someone I'd known for my whole life. This time with her was freedom contained in a capsule of this single night. I teased her nipples through the lacy silk and finally unclasped her bra.

I lifted my head from where I'd been making love to the sweet curve of her neck. Her breath was coming fast, her breasts rising and falling with her ragged gulps of air. Her nipples were deep pink and damp from my attentions. I trailed my knuckles over them lightly, loving how she flexed into my touch and the passion-drowsed look in her eyes.

I dipped my head and tasted one of her nipples without anything between us. *God.* She had this musky, slightly sweet flavor to her as if someone had sprinkled sugar on her skin with a dash of salt. She let out a sharp cry when I grazed my teeth over her nipple as I drew away. I made my way down her body, blazing a hot trail of kisses over her belly and roughly dragging her panties off.

I heard the rumpling of silk as they fell on the floor when she kicked them free of her ankles. I kissed the insides of her thighs, and she trembled beneath me when I trailed my fingers through her slippery wet folds. I needed to taste her. I sank two fingers inside just as I brought my mouth down. She bucked her hips roughly into my touch, crying out. I meant for this to take a while, but it didn't. Only two more strokes of my fingers inside her as I swirled my tongue around her clit, and then she shuddered roughly. I'd never once cared if someone cried my name, but I loved hearing it in her raspy twang.

I rose up, taking a moment to simply look at her. Fuck, she was glorious. Her skin was flushed and dewy, her eyes wide and her dark hair a tangle on the pillows behind her. She looked like a fallen angel, something pure and jaded about her. I wanted to know all of her secrets and unveil them one at a time until she was mine.

*Mine?*

I wasn't thinking clearly and gave myself a shake. I stood, finally unbuttoning my jeans. It was then I realized I had not planned for this moment. Not at all.

Madison must've read my expression because she asked, "What?"

"I don't have a condom," I said bluntly as we stared at each other.

She cleared her throat. "I have an IUD. I haven't been with anybody for over a year, and I can assure you I'm clean." Her voice went from husky to crisp as she spoke.

I wasn't ready to fess up that I hadn't been with anybody in over two years, but what the hell?

"Since we're being honest, it's been two years for me." Madison's eyes went wide, and I shrugged. "Single father and all that, small town. Everything's complicated."

There were many things I didn't trust. I wouldn't say I trusted Madison in the sense that I knew her story and I knew everything about her. I *knew* she had secrets, but in this, I trusted her completely. There was something too practical about her. She lifted her chin, holding my eyes.

"Get over here," she murmured with a crook of her finger.

That hint of bossy was another sharp spur in my desire, which was already rampaging out of control. My jeans joined hers on the floor in less than a second, and I was sinking down over her. I wanted her to ride me. So, I rolled over swiftly, shimmying back on the bed until I was propped against the pillows. She sat astride me with her hair falling in midnight waves around her shoulders, and her nipples playing peek-a-boo through the locks. I slid my hands down her sides, over the sweet dip of her waist and the lush curve of her hips.

"It's your turn," I said gruffly.

I thought I was in control. I really did. But then, she rose, reaching between us, and I felt the slick kiss of her core followed by the slow slide inside her rippling, silky clench. My head thumped back as I let out a ragged groan. "Holy hell."

I almost came instantly, but I gritted my teeth and clung to my control.

———

Opening my eyes, I took in the sight of her. Her dark lashes swept against her cheeks, and she bit the corner of her lip. She held still, her breath coming in sweet little pants.

"Look at me, sweetheart," I murmured. I gripped her hips tightly, pressing my fingers into the luscious give of her flesh.

Those lashes lifted, and her eyes met mine. I nudged a little deeper into her, and she blinked, shuddering a little. Then she rose again, sinking down and bringing me into her sheath. I felt her body tightening, her pussy rippling around my cock. She rocked again, just a little nudge, and then I felt her entire body tremble. My own release slammed through me so hard and fast it was like a whipsaw. Then it was all over but for the shudders. She fell against me, her head dipping into the curve of my neck. I held her body against mine, stunned at the force of my own release.

Even more, I was shocked at just how much I didn't want to let go of her.

# MADISON

Graham held me against his body, and I felt something I'd never felt before—comfort and safety. I also felt really, *really* incredible. I was beyond satiated. This man had just given me two climaxes in the span of half an hour. I considered that a miracle. But that wasn't what gave me comfort. It was resting in his strong embrace against every inch of his delectable rugged body and the gentleness with which he held me.

My heart cast out rushed beats, and I tried to pull it together.

I didn't remember falling asleep beside Graham. All I knew was it happened. Sleep didn't come easily to me. It never had. Yet with him holding me close, I tumbled into a dreamless, warm sleep without my usual restless thinking while anxiety ran laps in my thoughts. I had no idea if he intended to spend the night with me, but I woke before dawn the following morning with him curled up behind me. I discovered spooning was the best thing ever.

I'd never considered myself much of a cuddler. Not that I had all that much experience with cuddling with anyone. My ex certainly hadn't been a cuddler, and he was the only man I'd spent the night with. Well, except for Graham now. His warm, muscled body was behind me with his knees hooked in the bend of mine. One of his big palms rested on my belly. I'd never thought much about my own softness, but in contrast to Graham, who was all rugged, raw muscle, I felt small and soft.

I loved being held by him like this. Almost too much. The moment felt fragile as if I'd lose the feeling as soon as reality intruded. I took a deep breath, and it was then I noticed his arousal nestled against my bottom. My body moved on its own, shifting back slightly and savoring the knowledge that even in sleep, this man's instinctual reaction to me was to be turned on.

I didn't think of myself as much of a flirt. Actually, that was a big fat lie. I'd done nothing but flirt in high school, except it was all a façade. I'd never quite gotten the hang of flirting in the genuine, easy sense. I'd been called a tease when I was younger. Lord knows how I became homecoming queen or why I even wanted to. More to the point, *why* was I thinking about that right now?

Way to ruin the moment. Insecurity suddenly swamped me, and I wondered if I'd been awful last night. My ex had slashed my confidence in that area. Not that I'd ever had much knowledge, to begin with, but he told me I was too inexperienced. He told me I needed to relax, again and again and again. I remembered thinking that lecturing someone about how they needed to relax was a surefire way to actually prevent *that* from ever happening.

I hoped I hadn't been too terrible last night. I hadn't thought at all with Graham. I hadn't thought about where to touch him or what to do because it had all simply happened in a wild rush. I didn't mean to wiggle my bottom, but I did. And then, I felt Graham come awake. I couldn't say exactly how I knew. It was a subtle sense of awareness and my own body reacting to his. It was as if our bodies knew a language we didn't, a language I didn't know. All I knew was I could feel my slick arousal between my thighs, and that was rather startling.

Another complaint from my ex: I wasn't wet enough, whatever that meant. Last night, I'd been dripping. Despite the insecurity chattering in my thoughts, I knew I'd been plenty wet. Graham had slid in so easily. I swallowed, feeling myself flush all over, my skin almost prickling and tingling from the heat of it.

The sound of Graham's voice rumbled against the back of my neck. "Madison." There was a hint of warning in his tone, and I couldn't help it. He spurred this little sassy part of me I wasn't even familiar with. I wiggled my bottom again.

"Madison," he repeated in his gruff tone.

Merely the sound of his voice sent heat pooling low in my belly. "What?" I asked, trying to make my voice sound flirtatious. It just came out raspy, the edges roughened from sleep.

I wiggled my bottom again, and this time, Graham's chest rumbled with a laugh. His palm slid up my belly to cup a breast. All joking was over then, and I let out a shameless moan when I felt the calloused surface of his thumb dragging over my nipple. It was already perked up, all happy to see him.

"You're dangerous, sweetheart," he murmured in my hair before I felt the brush of his lips on my neck and the light graze of his teeth.

I'd never had morning sex. I'd always felt too insecure about how I looked. Graham had no such qualms. In fact, I discovered him to be bossy in the morning. He made love to my neck, and I never knew that just hot kisses and nips on my earlobe could leave me a melted puddle of a girl. All I wanted was him.

He rolled me over, catching both of my hands with one of his. He did have big hands, but wow, it was *so* freaking hot to be handled like that. Next thing I knew, he'd reached between my legs, murmuring, "That's my girl," when he found me wet and ready.

The moment his fingers disappeared, I let out a protesting whimper. His response? "Don't worry, sweetheart, I'll take care of you."

Dear God. *This* man. Take care of me, he did. He teased me to a fast climax with his fingers before filling me with his hot, thick length. I had my first quickie and came in a noisy burst a second time as he cried out roughly and shuddered against me. Moments later, as we lay on the bed in a tangled, sweaty heap, his hand trailed down my belly. No finesse, just a rough caress.

Wilbur startled us when I was recovering. I heard the click of his claws on the floor and looked over to see his cheerful face peering over the edge. A second later, he disappeared, and I listened as he walked out of the room again.

Graham chuckled. "Surprised he just showed up now." He rose on his elbow, and I opened my eyes to find him looking at me as if I were some kind of puzzle.

"What?" I asked, my insecurities punching through my passion-induced daze.

"You're gonna kill me," he murmured.

"What do you mean?" I pressed.

"You, sweetheart. You're dangerous."

With that enigmatic comment, which I thought he meant in a good way, he rolled off the bed swiftly. "Mind if I use your shower?" he tossed over his shoulder as he walked bare-ass naked across my bedroom.

Jesus, this man. Even the back of him was delicious. His back was all ropey muscles and his ass was tight. I wanted to squeeze it. I was pretty sure I had last night, but last night was all a blur, just a tumble of sensations, one rolling into the next, and me feeling desperate for Graham.

"Of course not," I said as I swung my feet off the bed.

The hardwood floor was cool under my feet, and I wiggled my toes as I stood looking down at the whimsical color. I suddenly recalled painting my toenails with Graham's daughter. I gasped, my hand flying to my mouth. I felt as if I had done something very naughty.

Graham turned around, and I saw the front of him. Gah! This man was way too comfortable with his body. He stood there completely naked with his cock still slightly swollen against his thigh. He arched a brow. "What?"

"Nothing." He remained silent, waiting. "Actually, I just remembered I painted my toenails with Allie."

Graham's brow rose a little higher, and he shrugged. "How about we not worry about that?" With that, he stepped in the shower, calling, "You can join me."

It was my shower, after all, or rather my grandfather's. That elicited another jolt of guilt. My grandfather was probably turning over in his grave. I just had sex in his old house. I shook my head as I walked into the bathroom, feeling bashful in my bare state.

Graham was standing by the shower with his arm stretched in to turn on the water. I lifted my chin, knowing that I probably had a full-body blush. "It's my shower, you know," I said, my tone crisp.

"I know that, Madison," he replied, his tone all gravelly and sexy.

Then he grabbed my hand and tugged me into the shower with him, where he proceeded to bring me to another climax. This was a record for me. Even my vibrator couldn't do this justice. I'd had some great orgasms with my vibrator, just not this many in such a short span of time.

After that, the awkwardness commenced. I had no idea how to do a morning-after with my new neighbor from Alaska, who was a hotshot firefighter and a gazillion miles away from what I thought my type was. Apparently, he was *my* specific type because no one other than him had ever turned me on like this.

"Would you like some coffee?" I asked a little while later. I'd walked Wilbur and fed him. We were dressed and in the kitchen.

"I'd love some." Graham glanced at his watch. "I need to pick Allie up inside of twenty minutes, and I don't have time to hit Firehouse first."

As I looked at him, I realized I'd actually given him a hickey. It was low and barely noticeable, right at the juncture where his neck met his shoulder. My face must have gone pink because he asked, "What?"

I gestured toward his neck. "I think I gave you a hickey."

"Seriously?"

I nodded.

"Fuck. This is the kind of thing Allie will notice."

I ran to the bathroom and brought out some cover-up. Of all the things I never thought I would do, this ranked high—helping a hotshot firefighter who'd driven me wild during the night and this morning cover up the hickey I'd given him.

As we stood by the door with Wilbur staring up at us like a chaperone, I suddenly didn't know what to say—me who prided myself on at least being able to use my manners to fake my way through any moment stared at Graham and blinked.

"Last night was incredible," Graham said, his voice low and gruff.

"It was?" I squeaked. Heat flashed up my cheeks.

"Sweetheart, it was," he said flatly. "Let's keep it between us, okay?"

When he dipped his chin, I felt my head bobbing. "Of course."

"Allie can't know."

"Right."

"And this town is the size of a thimble. If anyone else knows, you can be rest assured she will find out eventually."

After he drove away, I realized I'd become his dirty secret in one night. I didn't know if that was good or bad. I thought it was probably bad. He was probably embarrassed to have anyone know he even wanted me, the homecoming queen who'd landed here because she'd lost everything.

## Chapter Nineteen

# MADISON

After Graham left, I tried to shake my negativity loose. My insecurities felt like crabs in a bucket as far as winning the battle of what I should be feeling bad about this morning. Underneath the familiar negativity was this teeny, tiny voice trying to point out that it sure seemed like Graham had liked being with me. Maybe it was okay. Maybe I didn't need to be irrational about him not wanting anyone to know about us.

It wasn't as if I had gone into last night thinking it was something special. Definitely not. I hated how bad I was at being casual.

Wilbur let out a sharp bark. I was standing in the kitchen with my hand resting on the counter while I stared out the window at nothing. Leaning down, I scratched behind his ears. "You're right. I need to focus."

Wilbur seemed to like that and trotted beside me as I went to fetch my laptop. I'd discovered the built-in bookshelves had a fold-out desk by the windows in the living room. It was the cutest thing. It folded out at one end, and I could look out the windows while I worked. It was perfect.

Tapping open my email, I let out a little sigh. I liked being busy and feeling productive. Work had been one area of my life I'd felt good about, and now I didn't even have that. I was accustomed to plowing through over fifty to one hundred emails in the morning. And now, I had a measly eight. I was coming to despise this whole online dance around applying for jobs. Automated emails were the thing. I knew them well because that was what we'd had in our company. On this side, they felt so impersonal and so cold. I assured myself that if I ever ran a business again, I would actually hire a human being to deal with that stuff, even if it was expensive. It was such a letdown to see the automated replies that I knew came from a system and not a human.

I let out a squeal when I realized I had an actual response from a company in Anchorage. "Yes, yes, yes!"

I pumped my fists in the air. I startled a rabbit, and it bounded quickly across the clearing between the trees. As I watched, I realized its brown fur was turning white. "Oh wow," I breathed, completely forgetting about my job situation for the moment. "You must be a snowshoe hare," I said through the window.

I thought perhaps the rabbit could hear me because it stopped and looked back at me. After a second, it hopped into the trees out of my sight. I blinked and brought my attention back to my laptop. I had an actual job possibility. They'd contacted my references, and I had more experience than anyone locally. They wanted me to come to Anchorage tomorrow.

"Oh my god, oh my god!"

I jumped up from my chair and ran a little lap around the couch. My heart was pounding wildly, and my hands were actually clammy. While I was confident about my job skills, I'd only worked in my family's company. This was crazy. I was going to have my first job interview. Wilbur was excited and followed me along my next lap around the couch. I ran down the hall to look in my closet.

At least, I had plenty of perfectly good clothes. As I was perusing my options, I realized I needed to reply to the email. I raced back down the hall, skidding to the desk, and sat down quickly. I had enough sense to open a document and type my reply, reviewing it several times before pasting it in and sending it.

I then returned to look in the closet and settled on a navy pantsuit. It was just a touch past the bland shade of navy to give it a hint of color. I remembered the advice I'd been given by one of my professors when I was getting my MBA. She'd said you didn't really want anyone to remember what you wore to an interview. You wanted them to focus on *you*. Her advice had been to avoid being too flashy or too blah. Not that I was that old, but over the years I'd been hiring people at my family's company, I'd learned she was right. I never remembered what people wore when they blended in; I only focused on the person and their qualifications. Considering that women, myself included, could spend lots of time worrying about what to wear, that advice saved me time.

Wilbur seemed to know I was feeling good, and he trotted everywhere I went around the house. Not that

I had that many places to go. I passed between checking on my laptop to see if I had other emails, to going back to my bedroom to recheck what I had settled on to wear.

At one point, I held my phone in my hand, the touch of it cool. It got warm as I stared at the screen. I wanted to call someone to tell them the good news, but I'd learned quickly that my friends in Houston only liked me because of my connections. My grandfather would've been excited for me, but he wasn't here. I didn't want to call my mother because she would probably lecture me about falsifying the books for my father. He hadn't spoken a word to me since his initial arrest. By virtue of being a white-collar criminal, he was cooling his heels on supervised release with all of his assets frozen and travel limitations keeping him in Texas.

After a few minutes, I decided I'd go to Firehouse Café. Janet would be excited for me. Maybe I could make some friends in this town soon. Maybe I'd even make friends at my new job. I left Wilbur at home after taking him out for a walk. Between thinking about my job, or my almost job, my mind kept spinning back to last night.

I was still rather stunned by all of it. I didn't know if it was me or if it was Graham, but wow. It had been crazy good. Just thinking about it made me flush all over. When I pulled up outside the café, I wasn't paying much attention. I practically skipped in because I was so excited to tell Janet my news. My shoes squeaked on the floor when I looked ahead and saw Allie and Graham at the counter. My eyes whipped up to the clock above the chalkboard menu. She must've just gotten out of school.

*Hello, awkward moment, here I come.*

Just as I was about to turn around and leave, Janet called, "Hey, Madison!"

Allie's ponytail swung as she turned, her eyes twinkling with her smile.

## Chapter Twenty

# GRAHAM

I knew Madison was here before Janet said her name. She was a force field. Or rather, Madison near me created a force field. It snapped and crackled while sparks sizzled like little bolts of lightning in the air. The hair on the back of my neck rose. This woman made me feel like an animal. My cells spun and tightened in anticipation as I braced to face her.

When Janet greeted her, Allie spun around and squeaked. I heard her rushing over to greet Madison. I steeled myself and took a breath, keeping my expression level and calm, or so I hoped. Allie had reached Madison and was already talking to her, something about a band.

I could never keep up with Allie and the trends she followed. Madison seemed to be following along, her head bobbing up and down as she cast a warm smile at Allie. It was impossible not to notice how Allie soaked up her attention like a sponge. When Madison finally looked my way, my eyes lingered on the slight flush on her cheeks.

The instant our eyes met, the memory of the way

she looked last night when she came as I was clenched inside her struck me like a crack of thunder. She'd been warm, her skin dewy. The mere recollection sent a shot of blood straight to my groin. Fuck me. I needed to get my shit together. I could *not* be standing around with my daughter and be turned on by our new neighbor whom she adored.

While I wrestled with myself, Allie looped her elbow through Madison's and was dragging her over to me. Janet smiled. "What can I get for you?" she asked Madison as she slid my coffee over and handed Allie her mint hot chocolate.

I'd probably been here in this very spot while Janet multitasked like this hundreds of times, yet every millisecond felt charged all because Madison was near me.

"I'll take a coffee," Madison began before pausing. "Actually, what do you suggest?"

"Do you want something sweet?" Janet asked as I handed her my money. Oblivious to my internal unrest, she counted out the change with her eyes on Madison the whole time.

"No, I don't like sweet coffee, just hot chocolate."

"You like your coffee dark, right?" I prompted, belatedly realizing I'd just given away a detail about my knowledge about Madison.

I felt my daughter's eyes on me, piqued with curiosity. "When I dropped Madison off the other night, she offered me coffee," I said, immediately deciding to explain. Madison *had* offered me coffee, but it was when I went to apologize for getting cranky with Allie. I just didn't want to get into that.

Madison's head bobbed in agreement. "I do like my coffee dark." She looked back toward Janet.

"Let me make you my special espresso."

"You have a special espresso?" I couldn't help interjecting. "I've never had that."

Janet rolled her eyes. "Yes, you have. I always give you my special espresso."

"What's special about it?" Beck asked as he walked in, catching the tail end of her reply.

Maisie was at his side and nudged him with her elbow. "It's the one where she puts in an extra shot with the melted dark chocolate."

"Have I gotten that before?" Beck looked affronted he didn't know this detail.

I didn't know either, so I didn't know what to think. Janet rolled her eyes, looking amongst us. "I don't usually share my secrets, so keep it quiet, please."

She started making Madison's coffee, and Allie looked over at Beck and Maisie. "Have you met our new neighbor?"

Maisie nodded, her curls bouncing. "How are you settling in, Madison?"

Madison smiled. "Pretty well. I have a good lead on a job, and I'm going to Anchorage tomorrow for an interview."

"What is it you do?" Maisie asked.

"I'm an actuary," Madison replied.

Maisie blinked, which was probably what I did. "That involves a lot of math, right?"

Madison nodded. "I love numbers. It's basically assessing risks and valuation and some accounting."

I silently wondered if I could ask her to help Allie with her math homework.

"If I ever need help with accounting, I'll call you," Maisie said.

Beck chuckled and commented, "That's definitely out of my league."

Madison shrugged. "Hey, fighting fires terrifies me, so thank you."

At that moment, Nate Fox and his wife, Holly, came walking in. We did introductions, and Madison got pulled away by Maisie and Holly while they were chatting.

I glanced at my watch, then looked at Allie. "We need to get going soon. I've got some errands to take care of, and we're having dinner at your grandparents'."

"Why do you always call them my grandparents?" Allie protested. "They're your parents, you know."

"I know, but they usually invite us to dinner because they want to see you," I said.

Allie rolled her eyes. "Let me say goodbye to Maddie."

She skipped over to where Madison was sipping her coffee at the corner of the counter and listening to something Holly was saying. I watched as Madison said goodbye to Allie. She looked over to me and waved.

I left with my daughter, feeling unsettled. I was uncomfortable with my train of thought. I wanted to find some excuse to tell Allie she should stay at my parents' tonight so I could have another night with Madison. That was plain crazy.

As soon as we were in my truck, Allie confirmed my worst fears. "I think you should ask Madison out to dinner," she announced as she clicked her seat belt into place.

I started my truck, studiously not even looking her way. I backed out, commenting casually, "We took her to dinner just last night."

"No, I mean on a date."

"I can't date our neighbor." I finally looked her way, my heart pinching at the hopefulness in her eyes.

"Why not? Pretty much everybody's our neighbor in this town."

"Not exactly. Madison is our closest neighbor now."

Even I knew this was a stupid point, but it was all I could think of at the moment.

Allie let out an annoyed sigh. "Why can't you go to dinner with her? I think you like her, and I bet she likes you."

"Because it would be complicated if it didn't work out."

Allie blinked at me, sadness flickering in her eyes when I stopped at a stop sign and looked over. For a second, I thought she was going to cry. I put my hand on her shoulder, and she shook it off quickly as she stared out the window. "You're being stupid, and you know it. I just wish you'd stop using me as an excuse for why you never have a girlfriend. It might be nice to have a woman around, you know."

Ah, hell. I cleared my throat. "You're not an excuse. You're the most important person in my life and a priority for me. I just haven't met anyone I wanted to date. I don't know Madison that well."

All of that was true, but I *knew* I was hedging, and I was pretty sure my daughter was onto me.

"She's really awesome," Allie said, her eyes whipping to me.

Her eyes were bright, glistening with the threat of tears. Fuck my life. Teenage hormones were no joke. They seemed to bring emotions to the surface hot and fast for my daughter.

"I know, hon," I said slowly.

I heard the sharp draw of her breath, and she looked away from me again. I wished I could fix everything for her. That was something they never warned you about before you had kids. I'd spent all of Allie's life trying to balance the desire to prevent her from ever experiencing hurt with the awareness that life wasn't like that, and it wasn't always going to be easy.

I tried to cut myself a little slack. Because, fuck, I'd only been eighteen when Allie's mother got pregnant. No one had time to prepare me for being a father. I'd stumbled into it. Every now and then, some of us at the fire station would get roped into doing talks at the high school on various safety topics. I'd been invited a few times by the local family planning clinic to talk about birth control when they did the sex ed class. I could say without any irony to the guys that they'd better be prepared to be a father if they weren't using birth control.

Every time I did those talks, I would get wide-eyed looks like I was crazy, then I would tell them my story. I didn't regret a second of my life with Allie, but I'd give just about anything to somehow fix the enduring loss she experienced where her mother was concerned.

We drove in silence for a few minutes, and then she said, "I'll be okay."

"I know you will." I reached over and gave her ponytail a light tug.

She rolled her eyes when I looked her direction again. "You don't always have to do that, you know."

"Ah, now I know you're feeling better."

She let out an aggravated sigh. She passed on the grocery store run, so I dropped her off at the house while I went to take care of errands.

That evening as I slowed to turn onto the road that led to my parents' house, she asked, "Do you know what Gram's making?"

"No idea. I'm sure it'll be one of your favorites."

"You actually make the best spaghetti."

"I do?" Compliments were few and far between with this one.

"You know you do."

"It's because I'm not trying to be healthy about it," I teased. "Your grandmother likes to keep the cheese to a minimum, but I go crazy with it."

When I stopped in the circular driveway at my parents' house, Allie glanced over. "Will you at least think about dating someone? Ever?"

It never ceased to amaze me how my daughter could hold on to a topic for hours. I shrugged.

"I don't want to pressure you about Maddie even though I think she's awesome and you guys would make a great couple. But I don't even think you *think* about dating. That's not good for you, Dad," my daughter said, her brow furrowing as she looked at me seriously.

"I don't have a lot of time for dating," I finally said.

She let out another sigh. She was really good at sighs, and being fourteen meant all kinds of sighs. I still didn't know how to interpret them all. I thought this one meant she was annoyed with me and thought I was kind of stupid.

"You know what I mean. I'm in high school, and I don't have *any* memory of you dating anyone."

"Well, I haven't," I said honestly. "I've been busy, and I like my life the way it is."

I knew I was stumbling a little with this, but I didn't know how to smoothly back out of this conversation.

Allie let out a doozy of a sigh. "Oh, my God. Whatever, Dad." She climbed out and then paused with her hand on the door as I dropped my keys into the empty cup holder. "I still think Maddie is awesome, and you're stupid to overlook her."

After navigating that gauntlet with my daughter, I walked into dinner with my parents. I loved my parents. I even liked my parents, but I should've been prepared. I hadn't even thought about the fact my mother had met Madison when she was at dinner with us. If I thought my daughter was on my case about dating, my mom was even worse.

She made a delicious stir-fry for dinner. Afterward, Allie went upstairs to do some kind of video game thing with her friends. My mother didn't waste a second of time once Allie was out of earshot. I was enjoying a late evening cup of coffee, and my father was reading the newspaper. He still liked to do it the old-fashioned way with an actual paper.

My mother looked at me from across the table. The second she smiled, I knew she was onto something. "So, Harold's granddaughter is your new neighbor." Her voice was bright and casual.

I kept my expression bland, or so I hoped. My head bobbed up and down. "You met her."

"Madison seems like a lovely girl."

"She's very nice," I commented noncommittally. I heard my father's paper rustle and looked up to see he had bent the top down and was eyeing me. There was a slight glint in his eyes. He looked from me to my mother.

"I wondered how long it would take you to get to that," he said to my mother. He went back to reading his paper with a chuckle when I rolled my eyes.

"What?" my mother protested.

"It's fresh meat for your matchmaking efforts," he replied without looking up.

"Mom," I warned. "Don't even start with this."

"Honey, I would just like you to find someone. I hate seeing you alone."

"Mom, I'm not alone. I'm a busy guy with a daughter."

My mother pursed her lips as she looked over at me. "You use Allie as an excuse."

"Oh, for fuck's sake," I muttered.

"It isn't necessary to swear," my mother interjected.

I groaned and took a big gulp of my coffee. "Allie said the same thing," I finally mumbled. She would talk to my mom about us, so there was no sense in avoiding that.

"She's a smart girl. And she shouldn't feel like she's your excuse."

"Mom, can we just leave it alone? If I meet someone and it feels right, it'll happen. I'm sure you'd be the first to say that I shouldn't rush into anything."

"Of course, I would say that. But you don't even *amble* into anything." She pursed her lips again, shaking her head in disappointment.

I was so grateful for my parents' support. Without them, I didn't know what I would've done when Alison bolted when Allie was only a month old. It was tough, really tough, and there had been a tussle for control between Alison's parents and me. They thought they should have custody. Fortunately, the court didn't even entertain that idea, but it had been tense, and my parents had been an immense help. They'd also stayed civil with Alison's parents despite what they'd tried to pull when Allie was a baby.

"Mom, just let it go, okay? Madison's my neighbor, and it's good to have a neighbor without any complications."

My mother ignored me. "I asked Janet what she knew about her."

My father chuckled, not even moving his paper.

"You knew she was going to do reconnaissance for you, right?"

"I did." I took a breath.

"She seems nice. She's an actuary. That means she's smart," my mother offered. "Janet has nothing but good things to say about her."

"I know." I resigned myself to getting through this conversation and wondered what my mom would do if she knew that I already knew Madison really well, biblically speaking, that is.

"Apparently, there were some issues with her family's company," my mother was saying.

I couldn't help it because I was so freaking curious about Madison. "What do you mean?"

My mother's lips twitched, and a knowing gleam entered her eyes at that. "Her father's facing charges for fraud, and she refused to cook the books for him. I don't know if she was actually the whistleblower, but the evidence she provided only bolstered the case against her father when the investigation began. All of her father's assets are frozen. According to Janet, Harold wasn't even on speaking terms with her mother, but Madison was close with him. We can overlook what happened with the family." My mother waved her hand in the air as if she had some kind of say about it.

"Jesus, Mom. You can't hold her accountable for what her dad did."

"I know, I know. I didn't mean to imply otherwise."

I heard the sound of Allie's feet coming down the stairs, and I looked at my mother, narrowing my eyes. "Don't bring up your matchmaking ideas about Madison in front of Allie, please."

My mother twisted her fingers in front of her lips as if turning a key. "I promise. Whether it's Madison or someone else, just think about what I said. Allie could use a woman's influence in her life."

"She has you," I said just as Allie came in.

She looked back and forth between us. "What?"

"We're just talking about planning for the school dance. I'll be chaperoning," my mother said.

Damn, my mother was slick sometimes. I'd begged my mom to handle the school dance chaperone gig in my stead. Bless her heart, she'd graciously agreed.

Allie shrugged. "Okay. I still think it's stupid we need chaperones What do they think we're gonna do?" she pressed.

I thought about what I'd done at my first high school dance and decided to hold my silence on the topic. I didn't get anybody pregnant until my senior year, but I'd sure been into finding hidden corners to make out any chance I had. School dances were awesome for that.

"Can we go? The controller here is being weird," Allie said.

I hadn't even heard my mother's reply to Allie.

"You got it." Usually, I might try to get her to hang out with my parents longer, but right now, I wanted to escape my mother's curiosity.

Once we were driving home, Allie chirped, "I heard Gram talking to you about Madison. See, I'm not the only one."

*Fuck my life.*

## Chapter Twenty-One

# MADISON

I resisted the urge to skip on the way out of the building after my interview at the energy company in Anchorage. I was officially hired, and I wanted to jump up and down and scream.

Numbers, lots and lots of numbers, and analysis. I couldn't freaking wait.

Even better, I didn't have to worry about hiding everything that happened with my dad. They actually followed up with one of my references who confirmed I'd been helpful in the investigation. They even told me they were pleased to learn I had high ethical standards.

When I finally got into my car, I let out a squeal, punching my fists one at a time into the air before leaning my head against the seat and laughing. I had a job, an actual job. They were completely comfortable with remote work. They only wanted me to come into the office one day a week. That would give me a weekly dose of the city, but otherwise, I didn't have to worry about a commute.

I was starting in three weeks. They wanted to time

my start with a new project. I'd been trying not to dwell on my worries about how my connection to my father's company would affect my employment prospects. I'd done everything I was supposed to do when it all came crashing down, but it was ugly and messy. I hadn't wanted to hide it, but I also hadn't known exactly how to approach it. I'd gone with the only approach that sat well with me, which was to be honest. In the interview, I brought it up myself. I'd been relieved they didn't try to skirt around it either.

As I started my drive back to Willow Brook, my initial elation gave way to an emotional sense of relief. I cried for a few minutes. All my life, I'd taken so many things for granted, but my financial security had probably been the biggest one. I hadn't realized what a privilege it was, and I'd been in a sheer panic over the last year.

Not because I thought I deserved to have things handed to me, but because I realized how much I simply expected them to be there. I swiped my tears away and snagged a tissue out of the glove compartment to blow my nose while I drove with one hand.

I glanced over at the empty passenger seat where Wilbur had accompanied me on the drive from Texas to Alaska and laughed through my tears. My little dog was my best friend, but he wasn't here to listen.

"At least now I have a job," I said in the silence of the car.

I had a house and a job, and that was all I needed to survive. I only hoped I could make some friends. I really wanted someone to celebrate with. With income in my future, I decided to splurge and go to Firehouse Café. I might even get some food.

I didn't even have anyone to text, except maybe Graham. Somehow, I doubted he wanted a text from me, but the urge was too powerful. I pulled over at a viewing spot and slipped my phone out of my purse. My thumbs hovered for a moment.

Me: *I have a job!*

As soon as I hit send, I felt silly. I climbed out of my car because the view was stunning. Every state had viewing spots on highways, but Alaska outdid itself. This one offered a view of Cook Inlet. A seagull called in the air, and I heard what I thought was the call of an eagle, a loud screech. When I looked up and saw the size of the bird flying along the hillside, I knew it was an eagle. They were massive birds.

I swallowed and took a deep breath. My heart was thumping along in my chest. I was still coming down from the high of getting through the interview and getting the job. Maybe now, I could feel competent again. Numbers never lied. They always told the truth. Well, unless someone was manipulating the books like my father.

The sun glittered on the water, like diamonds cast on its surface. I saw a white form rise above the surface before dipping below. Another and then another followed. I knew I was seeing a water creature of some kind, but I didn't know what.

I watched for a few more minutes and then aimed back for my car. After a quick internet search, my best guess was I'd just seen a pod of Beluga whales. "Wow," I murmured.

Shaking my head, I started my car. I had a plan. After my little celebration at Firehouse, I would go home and start some homework. I couldn't wait to get my hands on all the numbers. I was buckling my seat belt when I heard the distinctive vibration of my phone as it rattled against the edge of the console.

Reaching down, I lifted it to see Graham had actually replied.

Graham: *Congratulations.*

He even included a balloon emoticon. I chuckled to myself.

Me: *Thank you. I didn't expect your emoticon savvy.*

His reply was swift.

Graham: *I have a teenage daughter. I have mastered emoticons.*

A high five followed by the winking emoticon came, and my belly swooped. I leaned my head back, feeling a little breathless. I was texting, for crying out loud, *texting* with this man, and I felt all fluttery inside.

Me: *Thank you for humoring me. I know you don't know me all that well, but it's kind of a big deal for me to get a job. I've been pretty stressed out.*

Now I was freaking confessing over text.

Me: *I'm sure you're at work. Sorry to bother you.*

Graham: *I am at work, but we're sitting here watching a fire burn.*

Me: *What?!*

Graham: *Don't worry, sweetheart. It's a controlled burn. Everything's fine. In fact, it's kind of boring. Back to your point. I think I know you pretty well, in some ways, that is. ;)*

Oh, gawd. My heart practically leaped out of my chest, and my belly spun wildly. Heat blasted through me, and I felt ridiculous.

Me: *Um, yes, I suppose you do.*

Graham: *;) Congratulations, jobs are good things to have. Can I call on you to help Allie with her math homework?*

I was smiling as I replied.

Me: *Anytime. I love math. Maybe it makes me a geek, but it's the truth.*

Graham: *Excellent. You're pretty much the opposite of a geek. I bet you were homecoming queen.*

When I saw his reply, I knew he was teasing, but my insecurities punched through my giddiness and elation and the fizzy desire that had sparked to life. I *had* been homecoming queen, and now I knew just how shallow it had been. For me, high school was nothing but trying to pull off being cool and failing inside every step of the way.

I took a deep breath and wished I had a different past. Looking back, it was embarrassing. Not that he was asking me, but I figured I might as well tell him the truth.

Me: *I actually was homecoming queen, not because I was the cool girl.*

Me: *Never mind.*

For the first time, he didn't reply right off. I wished I could see his face because I'd bet he thought that was stupid.

Graham was authentic, in every way. Even though he was handsome as sin, and I was sure all the girls wanted him in high school, he was not the kind of man who would fall for a shallow, silly girl who didn't know better. After a long moment when I had to watch the little dots taunting me, his reply came in with a buzz.

Graham: *I was kidding, but I suppose that shouldn't shock me. You're beautiful. Of course, you were homecoming queen. I like you as a math geek better.*

For some reason, my eyes stung with tears. My throat felt thick when I swallowed. I was so grateful he wasn't here to see me falling apart over a stupid text conversation.

Me: *I was a terrible homecoming queen, but I'm really*

*good at math. I'll let you get back to work. Please do text if Allie needs a ride or help with math.*

Graham: *Talk soon.*

He followed that with a series of emoticons, each one more ridiculous than the last, and lightness gusted through me as I laughed.

## Chapter Twenty-Two

# MADISON

A short while later, I looked up at the chalkboard mounted on the wall behind the counter at Firehouse Café.

"Should I try the turkey cranberry brie sandwich or the spinach feta pinwheel?"

I looked at Janet, and she looked back at me, her lips twitching with a smile. "Well, what are you in the mood for? The turkey one is sweeter."

"I think I'll take the spinach pinwheel. I love feta. Actually, I love all cheese."

Janet chuckled and called out my order to whoever was in the kitchen behind her. After that, she prepped me a coffee. "This is the first time you've ordered lunch here," she observed.

"I got a job," I whispered-shouted as I leaned across the counter, unable to keep my lips from stretching into a gleeful smile.

"Oh, this calls for a hug."

She rounded the counter, and before I knew it, I was enveloped in her warm embrace. She smelled like sugar cookies and cinnamon, and her hug felt so good

I almost burst into tears. I gave her a tight squeeze as I gathered myself together.

"Thank you," I said when I stepped back. "I kind of needed that.

"Anytime." Janet returned to the other side of the counter.

"Janet gives the best hugs," a voice said.

I glanced over my shoulder to see Maisie and another woman approaching. Maisie stopped beside me. "What's the hug for?" she asked.

"I got a job, and I'm super excited," I explained.

"Awesome!" Maisie lifted her hand in a high five, and I tapped my palm against hers. "This is Paisley," she said, gesturing with her chin, her brown curls bouncing as she did.

"Nice to meet you. Your names almost rhyme," I observed.

The woman beside her nodded. Maisie caught Janet's eyes when Janet handed over my coffee. "Paisley, this is Janet. She owns this joint and gives the best hugs. If you're having a bad day, come here. You should charge for those, you know," she said, looking toward Janet.

Janet flashed a quick smile. "Nice to meet you."

"You must be new to town," I commented. "Everyone who's from here knows Janet. I've only been here a few weeks, and I feel like I've known her forever."

Paisley laughed. "I just got here yesterday. I got hired on with the new hotshot crew."

"You're a hotshot firefighter?" I couldn't keep the surprise out of my voice.

Paisley's lips twitched with a quick smile. "I am. I love it."

"Women are the best firefighters," Maisie said with

confidence. "Trust me, I know. All the guys tell me women are the best under pressure. Graham will be your superintendent, and he rocks."

"Oh, I know Graham. He's my neighbor," I offered.

"He seems like a good guy," Paisley said. "I hope most of the guys don't mind having a woman on the crew. I can already tell Russell isn't thrilled."

The bell jingled above the door, announcing the next customers. "Oh, hey," Maisie said.

Our heads swiveled collectively in the direction of the door and back. Beck, who I recalled as Maisie's husband, entered with another guy and strode immediately to Maisie's side. He dusted a kiss on her temple. He held a toddler in his arms, and the little boy wiggled, thumping his feet on Beck's thigh. "Mama!"

Maisie leaned over and tousled the little boy's hair. She glanced at Paisley, then me. "This is our oldest, Max."

"Have you met Russell?" Beck asked, glancing from me to the man with him.

I'd discovered men in Alaska were, well, manly, and this guy was no exception. He was tall and fit with dark blond hair and brown eyes. "I don't think we've met. I'm Madison."

"Russell Dane." He dipped his head in acknowledgment.

"You must be a firefighter," I offered. I knew with certainty this had to be the Russell that Paisley had just been referring to. Whether she would admit it or not, I could practically feel the chemistry between them sparking in the air.

"I am," he replied, his tone low. His eyes flicked to Paisley. "Good to see you."

"And you," she said politely. "Well, I need to get going," she added, seemingly out of nowhere.

I knew by the flicker of confusion in Maisie's eyes that she had no idea Paisley had anywhere to go. "Don't you want to get some coffee first?" she asked, a glint of mischief following that flicker of confusion.

"I'll have to get some next time. I forgot I have an appointment." Before anyone could add anything, Paisley dashed out of the café.

Maisie shrugged. "Sit with me," she said to Beck. "Janet, can you get Beck his usual?"

"I want the special espresso that I didn't know was special," Beck added.

Janet rolled her eyes. "I know that's your usual."

After Russell ordered, they moved over to a small table. Just as I was about to take that moment for a graceful exit, Graham's mother came walking through the door. Janet brightened.

"Have you met Graham's mother?" she asked as his mother stopped beside me.

"Oh yes," Rose replied cheerfully. "I met her the other night. She was having dinner with Allie and Graham." She looked toward me. "Allie is glad to have a neighbor again. She misses Harold. He was only here half the year, but they got to be friendly."

"I miss him too," I said softly, feeling a pang in my chest.

"I'm sure you do." Rose's expression softened. She looked at me expectantly as if I might have something to add, but I didn't.

"How are you liking Willow Brook?" she asked next, a brightness to her voice.

"I love it so far. It's definitely a change of pace."

"From Houston?" she prompted. As soon as she

said that, I knew she'd had a conversation with someone about me.

"Yes," I offered politely. I *did* like it here, and if my job worked out, I could imagine staying here.

"What made you pull up stakes and come here from Houston?"

"I wanted a change of pace. When my grandfather left me his place, it seemed sort of like a sign." All of that was completely true if perhaps shading it as benignly as possible.

Another group of customers came in, effectively cutting off the conversation. I was relieved. I felt like Rose was trying to assess my intentions toward her son. I didn't know if she was trying to play matchmaker or scare me away. All of it was complicated by that smokin' hot night with Graham.

Even if I knew it was a crazy bad idea, I couldn't help but want more. My body just couldn't turn off the little engine of desire humming inside. I gave myself a mental shake and decided to enjoy my sandwich to go. Just then, Janet called over, "Did you want this to go or for here?"

"To go, please," I chirped from where I'd been waiting quietly at one end of the counter.

I managed to escape without any further questions from Graham's mother. When I arrived home, I took Wilbur for a walk before I enjoyed my spinach pinwheel. Then I settled in to do a little background work on the company that had hired me. I wanted to be ready to hit the ground running when I started. When my phone rang, I glanced at the screen to see the number for the Houston prosecutor's office.

Swallowing, I steeled myself, figuring I might as well take this call. Taking a deep breath, I closed my laptop and answered the phone. "Hello."

"Hi, I'm calling for Madison Glen."

"This is she."

"Hi, Madison. This is Harry Dan. If you recall, we spoke a few months ago about your father's case."

"I do recall. I was wondering when I might hear from you again."

"I was hoping we could talk about whether you're willing to provide a deposition."

My stomach knotted, and my chest felt tight, but I had no doubts about my answer.

"As I told you before, I would be willing to do that. I'm very sorry this is where it's ended up."

"I'm sure you are. This can't be easy for you."

"It definitely isn't, but I appreciate your understanding. Now, maybe we can talk about what you'd like to cover so I can be prepared. Also, if you're not aware, I've relocated to my grandfather's home in Alaska. If necessary, I could travel, but if we could do this over video conference, that would be preferable."

"That works fine. Now, let's get down to the details."

After a long two hours, I stood from my computer after ending the call and walked over to stare out the windows. I was exhausted emotionally and mentally. I was a key piece in the case against my father. I would be able to confirm the irregularities because I had kept all the original records. I hated being in this position. Turning away from the windows, I plunked down on the couch and kicked my feet up on the coffee table.

Wilbur promptly jumped up on the couch beside me. I scratched along his neck as I leaned my head back. I really wanted a glass of wine and maybe a bath. That would be ideal.

Standing, I crossed to the kitchen and poured that glass of wine before deciding to look into starting a fire. My grandfather had left a stack of wood in the small rack by the fireplace. I wanted to enjoy this wine with a fire. Maybe I could metaphorically burn away my worries. An hour later, I was still staring at the fireplace.

"It can't be this hard."

I looked at the logs, letting out a deep sigh just as my phone vibrated over on the coffee table. Turning, I scooped it up to see a text from my hot neighbor.

Graham: *Allie wants to know if you'd like some pizza.*

Of course I wanted pizza. Maybe Graham could help me start the fire.

Me: *I'd love some. If you can come over and start a fire for me, I'll cover the pizza. We can eat here if that's okay.*

## Chapter Twenty-Three

# GRAHAM

I chuckled as I read Madison's text. She needed me to start a fire. I could absolutely handle that. I was feeling uncertain about the pizza, though. Actually, it wasn't the pizza. I was unsettled about seeing Madison at all. But Allie wanted to have pizza with her, and Allie was the ideal chaperone.

We could have pizza and then leave. Allie had no slumber party tonight, so I didn't even need to worry about anything happening afterward. It was a safe plan, so I tapped out my reply.

Me: *Sure thing. But I'm buying. We'll be there in about 20 minutes. Any preferences for pizza?*

Madison: *Pepperoni if you and Allie like that. Otherwise, I'll take whatever you like.*

Me: *Uh, we love pepperoni.*

I was actually surprised she liked pepperoni. That didn't seem to fit with a former homecoming queen. I'd been wrestling with that. Allie's mom had been homecoming queen. For some reason, I'd held that against her even though I'd been homecoming king.

Probably because that was how I ended up lusting after her so badly.

We'd been paired together for a series of events. She'd been young and beautiful, and I'd been young and looking for fun.

Madison was different, or maybe not. She was more than beautiful—sultry and stunning. I doubted Allie's mom could start her own fire. Whatever. It was useless to have these mental debates with myself.

I set my phone down and looked ahead to see Allie coming out of the grocery store. We needed milk, and she'd volunteered to run in and get it. She slipped into the front seat, buckling up and setting the gallon of milk between her feet on the floor.

"Are we getting pizza with Maddie?"

"We're picking it up and going to her place."

"What kind does she want?"

I cast a quick grin as I backed out of the parking space. "Pepperoni."

"Oh, she has my same favorite!"

My daughter clapped her hands, and I bit back a groan. "Don't get any ideas," I muttered as I started driving toward the pizza place.

When I slid my gaze sideways, I caught a dramatic eye roll, followed by an annoyed sigh. Allie didn't dwell, though, and commented, "I get to see Wilbur. He's so cute!"

"No argument there," I offered.

In short order, we were turning down Madison's driveway after picking up the pizza. Allie was practically bouncing in her seat with two boxes of pizza on her lap. "Do we need to bring the milk in?" she asked once I parked.

"Nah, it's plenty cold out."

Wilbur greeted us with a bark on the other side of

the door before Madison swung it open. I braced myself for the impact. As soon as my eyes collided with hers, it felt like a jagged bolt of lightning ripped through the air between us. My entire body sizzled, and I took a quick breath. Madison's eyes bounced away.

"Hey! We have two pizzas. Dad eats a whole pizza, so you and I can split the other," Allie offered cheerfully.

Madison laughed as she opened the door wider. Wilbur was busy circling our feet, and she caught my eyes again. "I hear you need help with a fire. Let's start with that."

As we walked through the entryway, she gestured to a neat stack of wood beside the fireplace. "I tried starting it, but I can't get it to light." She bit her lip, and I forced my eyes away from lingering on it. "It's silly. I should know how to start a fire."

Allie chimed in, "I didn't know until Dad taught me, and that was just last year. Plus, it's cold in Alaska, and you're from Texas. I'm guessing you don't need fires down there."

Madison cast her a grateful smile. "No, it's pretty warm there."

I crossed over, eyeing the stack of wood. It needed to be split, and she also needed some kindling. "Do you know if Harold left an ax or a maul?"

Madison nodded. "There's an ax in the storage area on the porch."

I walked out onto the front porch, silently lecturing myself. Even if my entire body revved at the sight of Madison biting her plump bottom lip and I viscerally recalled the feel of her flying apart in my arms, I told myself she was not a practical girl, not the kind of girl I should fall for. I already knew lust was no path to love. Not to mention, I wasn't even looking for love.

After I found the ax, I returned inside to fetch the wood. "Be right back. Why don't you two start eating?" I called over my shoulder.

I heard Allie asking Madison where the plates were and then their footsteps as they made their way to the kitchen when I walked outside. With a quick scan of the nearby trees, I discovered an old stump off to the side of the circular driveway where Harold chopped his wood. I quickly split the small armful of wood. After Madison found some old newspapers to use for kindling, I had a fire started in no time.

I returned outside and split more wood from the small pile Harold must've left behind. When I came back inside, Allie and Madison were already eating in the living room.

Allie paused between bites. "Go get your pizza. It's on the kitchen counter, and there's a plate for you. You can have ginger ale, orange soda, or water."

"You happen to have a beer?" I asked, glancing toward Madison.

"I do. Check the fridge and help yourself. I didn't offer Allie a beer." At that, Allie rolled her eyes.

"I figured as much," I said dryly.

A few minutes later, I was back in the living room. Allie was sitting in the corner of the sectional while Madison sat on one side, and I sat on the other at an angle across from her. The distance should have forced the lust racing in electrical cycles through my body to slow down. No such luck. With Madison sitting across from me with one foot tucked under her knee, every subtle motion she made drew my eyes to her.

Her dark hair was pulled high on her head in a ponytail, and I wanted to slide it loose and wind it around my hand. I could imagine doing precisely that and giving it a hard tug as I sank into her from behind. That vision came to me after she had gone to the kitchen and then returned, bending over to check on Wilbur and giving me a most excellent view of her heart-shaped bottom.

Allie—hopefully oblivious to the thoughts spinning through my mind—chattered about a few things at school and asked Madison's opinion on hair dye. "You're not dyeing your hair," I interjected when I kicked through the haze of lust clouding my thoughts.

"Why not?" Allie countered, looking affronted.

I sighed. "Uh, you're just not."

I saw the twitch of Madison's lips, but she tightened the corners and managed to keep from smiling. I was feeling contrary, if only because I was annoyed at how easily Madison affected me. "Don't you agree?" I pressed when I caught her eyes again.

"About what?" she asked, her tone light.

"Don't you think she's too young to dye her hair?"

Something flickered in Madison's eyes, and she lifted her chin slightly, straightening where she sat on the couch. She finished the last bite from a slice of pizza and set her plate down before replying. "Actually, no. There are so many options for hair dye these days. She can do something temporary, and it'll wash out within a week."

I blinked at her, surprised she'd disagreed with me. Meanwhile, Allie grinned. Wilbur jumped up beside her, and she leaned down to nuzzle his face and scratch behind his ears before looking up at me. "See, I told you it's not a big deal."

"I'll think about it," I grumbled. "But only something temporary."

Now, Allie cast me a sly grin. "Absolutely. Just

something temporary. I don't want anything permanent anyway because what if I hate it?"

"Exactly," Madison agreed. "You never know how it looks until you try it."

I was relieved when they kept chatting as I finished off my pizza and beer. A few minutes later, I was in the kitchen, rinsing my plate and closing up the pizza boxes. I felt Madison enter the room. The hairs rose on the back of my neck and along my forearms. My body knew her. I felt like a weathervane turning toward her. She crossed over, stopping next to me and setting her plate on the counter.

"You don't need to clean up. You bought the pizza." She looked up at me, and for a second, I lost myself in her green eyes. There were layers of color, like a ray of sun shimmering into the ocean. My cock was so hard, I ached for her.

I stuffed my hands in my pockets to keep from kissing her senseless with my daughter only one room away. "Okay," I replied, my voice coming out gruff. I cleared my throat and swallowed. "We'll get going soon."

"Thank you for starting the fire. You must think I'm silly," she replied.

Her lips tilted into a lopsided, self-deprecating smile. I'd been trying to convince myself she was shallow and impractical. Just now, I felt a sharp twinge of guilt.

Shaking my head, I said, "Now you know how to start a fire. I split enough wood for a few days for you."

"I saw that. Thank you."

My fingers curled in my pockets, literally itching with the urge to reach for her. Suddenly, Allie was there, and I practically jumped at the sound of her voice.

"That was so good. Thanks for letting us stop by." She walked across the kitchen with Wilbur trotting behind her.

Madison turned away from me, and I didn't even hear what they were saying while I wrestled to kick my dirty thoughts to the curb. This was a new problem for me. As a single father, I hadn't found it difficult not to date. Oh, sure. I was a healthy man with sexual needs, but the occasional passing interaction was enough to keep me satisfied. But no one, *no one*, had ever distracted me the way Madison had.

If I was being honest, I knew I was in deep. I needed to remember to be sensible. We left, and I drove home. Later that night, I had to take matters into my own hands in the shower. My climax hit me hard as one palm rested against the tile with my head bowed. What a waste of an orgasm. Especially when I knew how much better it was with Madison.

## Chapter Twenty-Four

# MADISON

After Graham and Allie left, I found myself lying in bed, staring at the ceiling above me. With the small night-light in the corner, I could just make out the knots in the wood. I counted them again and again, trying to determine if they formed anything resembling a constellation.

It didn't help derail my train of thought. I couldn't stop thinking about the look in Graham's eyes in the kitchen—that dark flicker of desire that sent fiery heat sliding through my veins. Without thinking, I was slipping my hand over my belly and dipping my fingers between my thighs to find myself slick with need for him.

After I brought myself to a quick orgasm, I felt unsatisfied. I knew just how much better it was with him.

I didn't see Graham for a few days—not at the coffee shop in town and not driving by on the road—but it didn't matter. He crowded every corner of my mind. I wanted to see him again, and I knew it wasn't practical. I knew he had to think I was ridiculous. The homecoming queen who didn't know how to start a fire. I was a quick study, though. Since he'd shown me how to start one, I'd had several fires in the fireplace. I'd also taught myself how to split wood.

One evening, with a fire snapping and crackling in the fireplace and Wilbur dozing on the floor in front of it, my phone vibrated. I glanced down to see a text from Graham.

Graham: *Mind if I stop by?*

My thumbs were typing out a reply before my brain could catch up.

Me: *Of course not.*

As soon as I hit send and lowered the phone, I smacked the heel of my hand to my forehead. *You never play it cool. It's ridiculous for you to seem so eager. He's probably just stopping by to...*

I didn't know why he was stopping by and couldn't come up with a benign reason. My hopeful hormones had an idea, though. *Maybe it's a booty call because we would totally love a booty call.*

I was a little worried. I'd never even been in a casual relationship at all. Except for Graham, I'd gotten engaged to the only other guy I'd done more than kiss. I leaned my head back with a groan, and Wilbur looked up from his perch. My phone vibrated in my hand again. I glanced down to see Graham's reply.

Graham: *Okay, be there in a few.*

I leaped up and dashed down the hallway, practically skidding into the bathroom. I flicked on the light and stared at myself in the mirror. Snatching a brush out of the drawer, I ran it through my hair quickly. I debated putting on a swipe of lipstick, but that seemed ridiculous. I was just hanging out at home by myself because that was basically all I did these days.

I heard a heavy knock on the front door. Eyeing myself critically, I shook my head. I was being silly for worrying about my appearance.

Wilbur let out a bark, and I heard the sound of his claws as he crossed to the entryway. Turning the light off in the bathroom, I forced myself to walk at a normal pace down the hallway. I didn't need to seem too eager. My pulse ignored my orders, beating out a wild staccato rhythm, the echo of it resounding through my body. I felt hot and tingly all over. When I reached the door, I forced myself to take a deep breath.

Another moment later, there was another knock, and I felt foolish. When I finally opened the door, my breath seized in my lungs, and my pulse skidded out of control. Sweet hell. Graham was just standing there. He had a hand hooked over the upper door jamb. With his arm lifted, his Henley shirt rose slightly. My eyes landed on the thin strip of skin exposed just above his jeans. I wanted to lean down and lick it. He was very lickable, *all* of him. Unfortunately for me, I knew he tasted good. My hormones were making a messy racket—overexuberant like an eager puppy—at the sight of him.

"Hi," I said, rather breathlessly.

"Hi." He was curt and not breathless.

His eyes swept over my face, dipping down and then back up. I wiggled my toes self-consciously. "Can I come in?" he prompted.

"Oh, right. Of course."

I stepped back, and Wilbur circled his ankles in greeting. My little heart swooned when Graham knelt to give him a proper hello, scratching him under the chin and letting him lick his cheek. My former fiancé had never loved Wilbur all that much.

Graham's kindness toward Wilbur was like catnip for my libido.

He straightened, and I opened the door wider. "You can hang your jacket up." I waved vaguely in the direction of the hooks on the wall nearby. Without a word, he shrugged out of his jacket and hung it. My eyes greedily soaked up the sight of his broad shoulders shifting under his shirt as he moved. He toed off his boots and followed me into the living room. His eyes landed on the fire and bounced to me as his lips curled in a slow grin. His grins were dangerous. This one sent my belly spinning.

"I see you started a fire yourself."

I nodded. "I even chopped the wood." I felt ridiculous as soon as I said that.

If Graham thought I was foolish, it didn't show. He nodded firmly as if he were proud of me. That gave me a little flush of pride followed immediately by that foolish feeling again. There were few areas in my life where I felt competent. Aside from my work, I'd felt like a desert of cluelessness over the past year. It hadn't helped to have my fiancé dump me and watch as the friends I'd thought were my friends blow away like tumbleweeds in the wind.

I took a breath. That wasn't my life anymore. I didn't need to worry about it. While I felt foolish and insecure around Graham about a whole host of things, I didn't worry at all that he cared one iota about my financial situation or my father's business and connections. He would probably find it hysterical that I'd once cared about it. I gave myself another mental kick. For crying out loud, all I could focus on was the negative.

I spun away, waving at the fire. "Thanks to you, I

know how to start a fire. Anyway," I said brightly, "what were you stopping by for?"

Graham suddenly looked uncomfortable when I turned to face him again. It was then I noticed he held a plastic bag in his hand. What with all his hotness distracting me, I supposed I could be forgiven for my weak powers of observation. He let it slide into his other hand as he opened it. He cleared his throat when he looked up at me, an endearing uncertainty entering his eyes. "Allie wants to dye her hair. I don't know if I got the right stuff."

He handed me the bag. "You want my help?" I pressed, unsure what he needed. "Is Allie with you?"

He shook his head quickly. "No, she's on a camping trip. She'll be back the day after tomorrow, and I wanted to surprise her." He gestured at the bag. "Did I get the right stuff?"

Peering inside the bag, I saw not one but four boxes of hair dye, the kind one would get at a pharmacy. I pulled a box out. "What color does she want?"

"She said burgundy and pink." Graham ran a hand through his hair.

"Have a seat," I said, gesturing to the couch.

The poor man looked lost. He sat down and rested his elbows on his knees when I sat down nearby. "Looks like you've got the right colors."

"Is that temporary?" he prompted.

I nodded. "Most everything you get at the drugstore is temporary, I promise. Even when it's done professionally, nothing's permanent. If it looks awful, it won't last very long so you don't need to stress."

"Should I have gotten something else for her?"

As I sat there, I mulled over what to say. In my old life, I used to spend a lot of money on my hair.

"You seem like the kind of person who would know about hair," he added as if he'd read my mind.

I shrugged. "Maybe." My stylist in Houston would've thrown these boxes away. I wasn't going to share that with Graham.

I couldn't believe I ever thought the brand of hair dye mattered. It was sweet that he got them for Allie, especially knowing he initially told her she couldn't dye her hair. "This will do the trick for her."

"But is it what you would get?" he pressed.

I brushed my hair over my shoulder, letting it slide over my hand as I lifted it. "My hair's really dark."

He cleared his throat, his eyes darkening slightly as his chin dipped. "Right. You have dark hair," he said, stating the obvious.

"My hair's not easy to color, so when I do it, I have it done professionally because they have to lighten it first and so on." I let my fingers slide through the locks as I looked back toward him.

"Allie's hair is brown."

"I know, but it's definitely lighter than mine. I'm sure these will work."

"Maybe I should try something different."

I shook my head quickly. Before I realized what I was doing, I put my hand on his thigh. "She should try this first. Stop worrying so much."

His shoulders rose with a deep breath, falling as he let it out in a whoosh. "Can you help her with this? This is out of my league."

"Of course I'll help." My heart squeezed tightly. This side of Graham, the uncertain father trying to help his teenage daughter dye her hair, was too sweet for words. He was a good man, the best kind of man.

He let out another sigh. "Thank you."

My hand was still on his leg, and I realized it in a

split second. The heat of his thigh radiated into my palm, and I couldn't bring myself to move it away even though I tried to tell myself I had to.

He had one elbow resting on a knee as he looked at me. I stared back at him, and I got lost in his dark gaze. It felt as if sparklers were going off inside my body, scattering heat everywhere and lighting little bonfires. I couldn't even speak. I was caught in the undertow of the currents of desire and need rushing through me.

Graham straightened. I sensed a shift in purpose, a deliberateness to him. "Madison," he began, his voice low and gravelly.

I swallowed nervously. "Yes?"

"I want you," he said so flatly my heart kicked at my ribs in response.

I tried to do something, to say something, but all I could do was stare at him. I felt as if I were unspooling inside—the restraint and control and sensibility that I usually kept buttoned around me was falling away, and I was spinning loose.

"You do?" I heard myself asking, my tone surprised.

His lips kicked up at one corner as he nodded slowly. "Very much." He paused, his eyes skating over my face. "I just want to make sure we're on the same page."

"Page?" What did pages have to do with this? Apparently, all I could do was ask questions.

"I can't really consider a relationship right now."

"Of course not. I understand," I heard myself saying. Because, of course, he couldn't. Especially not with me, the impractical girl I was. "I'm not looking for a relationship."

That *was* true, insofar as I hadn't expected to even

want anyone, much less be faced with this wild rushing desire I felt for Graham.

"Okay then. Allie wants us to date."

"She does?" I chirped. There I went with another question.

He nodded slowly. "She does."

"I'm not sure what you're saying."

"I'm saying that I want you more than is sensible, and I don't want to create the wrong impression for my daughter."

"Okay." I was still a little confused.

"I guess I'm saying let's play it by ear, but I didn't want you to have expectations."

"Okay."

Wow. I was a brilliant conversationalist tonight.

"I have a question, though," he added.

"What's that?"

"Do you want me?"

His gaze was like a beam, and I couldn't look away. My insides went molten. I blinked and took a shallow breath. "Yes," I whispered.

"Well, that's good then."

"It is?"

His lips stretched from one corner to the other in a delicious grin that had butterflies amassing in my belly when he nodded. I could feel the slick arousal between my thighs.

Then he was reaching for me and pulling me onto his lap. Oh. My. God. Graham's lap was the best thing ever. I could feel his muscled thighs and the press of his arousal against my bottom. His chest was perfect to rest against as he palmed my cheek and turned his face toward mine. On the heels of a shallow breath, his lips brushed mine, and then I was falling into one kiss after another. They were hot and overpowering.

Graham simply devoured my mouth once his tongue swept inside.

I couldn't get enough, pressing close to him, kissing him almost frantically and pouring the need storming through my body into our kiss. Our tongues dueled, and his palm slid from my cheek to cup a breast. He broke free from my lips, murmuring, "Fuck, you're gonna kill me."

"I am?" I was breathless with that question.

His eyes were dark and knowing as he held my gaze. "Absolutely. In all the best ways."

With his molten eyes on me, he hooked his fingers on the hem of my shirt and tossed it aside quickly. I shivered under the feel of his calloused palms as one coasted over my belly and the other cupped my breast, his thumb brushing across my tight, achy nipple. He dipped his head, the heat of his mouth closing over my nipple. He gave it a sweet suck, and I cried out at the light graze of his teeth. He lifted his head, murmuring hot, filthy words over my skin as we kissed and touched while our hands and lips wandered over each other.

Somehow, I got his shirt off and unbuttoned his jeans, letting out a happy hum when I curled my palm around the velvety heat of his shaft. It was hard and pulsed under my touch. I loved how he let out a groan, murmuring, "Fuck, Madison."

I shimmied back to kneel before him. I smeared my thumb across the tip of his cock, swiping up the drop of cum rolling out. I was feeling sultry and saucy, and I lifted my thumb to lick it clean.

Graham's eyes went even darker as he watched me. "Madison." His voice was verging on a growl. His eyes encouraged me to keep going. I dipped my head, dragging my tongue along the underside of his cock, loving the feel of his hand tangling roughly in my hair when I circled my tongue around his thick crown. I savored the salty, musky taste of him as I brought him fully into my mouth and sucked him deep. I loved how his hand tightened in my hair, causing a sting on my scalp. Lightly cupping his balls, I settled in to try to drive him maybe just as wild as he drove me. I was having fun, enjoying having him at my mercy.

He gave my hair a tug, followed by a gruff command. "Come here."

I lifted my head, licking my lips as I looked at him from where I knelt in front of him. He moved swiftly, standing from the couch and spinning me around. My leggings were yanked down and tossed aside. I loved the way he handled me—kind of rough and bossy, but always on the edge of gentle.

Before I knew it, my knees were sinking into the couch, and his hand slid down my spine. The heat of his touch sent cinders scattering as his palm moved through the dip of my spine and over the curve of my bottom. I felt the velvety brush of his cock on the insides of my thighs when his fingers teased between them.

"Oh, sweetheart, you are so wet." This was followed by a satisfied growl when two fingers slipped in easily.

I let out a moan as I pushed back into his touch. "That's my girl," he murmured. I felt his lips dropping kisses like warm honey down my spine while he teased and pumped in and out of me with his fingers.

I was near incoherent in my begging. "Graham, please. I need—" I cried out when he buried his fingers deep inside me.

"What do you need, sweetheart?"

"You. More."

"You got it."

Finally, *finally*, I felt the thick press of his cock at my entrance, followed by the slow glide. My head fell forward. I savored the way his fingers dug into one hip as he held me. He buried himself fully, rocking in subtle nudges as if to seat himself completely. I felt his hand slide up my spine again, lacing into my hair as he wound it around his hand.

He fucked me. Hard. And I loved every single second of it. The tug on my hair, the pull and glide as he thrust into me again and again. I was frantically chasing my release, and everything was spinning inside a storm of sensation. Just when I thought I couldn't topple over, he released my hair and reached around my waist, pressing his fingers over my slippery swollen clit. Pleasure burst in a ray through me as I shuddered roughly, grateful for his strong hold on me.

I felt him draw back once again, as he said something unintelligible, and then the heat of him filling me as he pulsed and jerked inside me.

He curled around me, and all I could hear was the thundering beat of my heart mingling with the sound of our ragged breathing. After a few moments, he shifted, lifting me easily.

He held me close as he sat down. I was curled in his lap while he was still buried inside me. I rested against him, feeling sated and replete and utterly protected in his embrace as his fingers sifted through my hair.

My treacherous heart loved every second of this. I tried to tell myself to be practical. But I was far past that, and I knew it.

## Chapter Twenty-Five

# GRAHAM

Madison sat on my lap, a dewy bundle of curves. With every breath, I inhaled her scent. Raw, elemental need had taken over. A small part of me wanted to believe it was just chemistry. There was absolutely no doubt it *was* chemistry. But it was also *more*.

As I held her, a sense of tenderness, strong and sure, stole through my heart. I didn't know what to do with Madison. I knew I wasn't ready to go home and tell my daughter I was dating anyone.

Despite my best intentions, Madison was more than a secret. No matter how much I tried to tell myself otherwise, she was more than a fling. For now, I was relieved beyond what should be sensible at the fact Allie was gone for two nights. Because unless Madison kicked me out, that meant I could have two nights with her. That was a luxury, pure and simple.

Somehow, we untangled ourselves and actually put on clothes. Madison offered me a beer while she had a glass of wine. We watched television. I held her against my side, my arm resting over her shoulders. She snuggled right in as if she belonged there.

Wilbur decided the other side of me was perfect for him, and I discovered he didn't like me to ignore him for too long. Madison laughed, offering, "He's ridiculously spoiled. Sorry. All you have to do is rest your hand on him every now and then, and then he doesn't get fussy."

I chuckled, and it was all so easy and felt so good. Later, I had her again. This time, we were tangled in her sheets with her legs curled around my hips. Afterward, I fell into a deep, dreamless slumber.

She didn't kick me out the next day, and I showed her a hiking trail nearby. It was an offshoot along the path that connected Harold's property to mine. He'd used it for hunting. It led through the trees to an open field in a valley with a glittering glacial river in the distance.

I spent the next night with Madison. Every minute of the weekend felt like stolen time, and I supposed it was. Allie had plenty of friends and loved slumber parties, but two nights in a row was not as common. This was the very first time I'd had two nights with any woman since Allie had been born. I didn't count the month with her mother because we hadn't once slept together.

As I drove into work after that second night, I shook my head, recalling the month after Allie came into the world. Jesus. It was weird to think about now. My parents had converted the space above their garage into an apartment for us. Maybe if we hadn't had a newborn, it would have been fun. I loved having a newborn baby, but it was nerve-racking and scary. Even though I didn't know she was about to walk away, I knew Allie's mom didn't like it. That month was a blur in my memory.

I took a breath, slowing as I turned into the

parking lot at Willow Brook Fire & Rescue. My crew was filled now. I had twenty-five people to manage. We'd done a few training exercises together, but this was our first week on call.

Rex had told me he had some dead trees for us to burn in an area on his property that had been hit hard with beetle kill. It was an ideal way to practice and close to town. As I strolled down the hallway at the station, I paused when I heard my name. Taking a few steps back, I peered through the door into a shared office. "What's up?" I asked.

Cade grinned, gesturing me in. "Close the door for a sec, if you would."

Stepping through, I closed it behind me. "Now you've got me worried," I added as I sat down across from him.

"Just thought I'd give you a heads-up that Russell and Paisley had a small spat, I guess."

"Spat?"

He shrugged. "Yep. I don't know what Russell said, I don't even know if he said anything, but she told him to stop being a sexist asshole. He told her that she'd have to prove to him she could handle the work."

I rolled my eyes, letting out a groan. "Are you fucking kidding me? I've known Russell for years. I've never seen him be a jerk about women."

"Me neither," Cade agreed.

We'd all grown up in Willow Brook together. "Want my two cents?" he asked.

"What do you think?"

"I think he's got a thing for her, and that's the problem."

"Fuck. I can't deal with an office romance. Is that what we should call it?"

Cade chuckled and shrugged. "They're sure not a

couple now. They wouldn't be the only couple, though. Susannah and Ward used to be on a crew together."

"I know, but they're married, and they have a baby," I replied.

"It wasn't that way at first. Maybe have a word with each of them. That's what I'd suggest."

I nodded. "Thanks for giving me the heads-up. I'm going to talk to him now. Anything else I need to know?"

Cade shook his head. "Not a thing. Dad is stoked you guys are doing that training burn on his property, though."

I grinned. "It's convenient."

He dipped his chin in agreement. "You guys are on the call rotation starting this week."

Tapping my knuckles on the armrest, I stood. "We are. Thanks again." On my way to find Russell, I swung through the kitchen to get some coffee. Once I had that in hand, I searched out Russell in the weight room and gestured to him. "I need a minute."

He set the weights down, and I could tell from the look on his face that he probably knew why I wanted to talk to him. I took him to one of the shared offices. The very Ward that Cade and I were just talking about, who was married to Susannah was just leaving. "Mind if I use it for a few minutes?" I asked.

"It's all yours. I'm headed over to grab some breakfast. Need anything from Firehouse?"

"Can you grab me a bagel and cream cheese?"

With a thumbs-up, he was gone, and a moment later, Russell appeared. I closed the door behind him, and we sat down at the round table.

"Let me guess, somebody told you I had an argument with Paisley."

I nodded.

Russell leaned back in his chair, wincing slightly. "I'm sorry. She gets under my skin. I know women are good firefighters, I swear."

"I know you do. I'm not sure what your deal is, but you need to clear the air with her. Is there anything I should know?"

He shook his head quickly. "I'll talk to her."

"I'm going to talk to her first, and then I'll let you two have the office. How's that sound?"

Russell let out a quiet sigh and nodded. After he left, I scouted out Paisley in the break room. As soon as I asked her to come meet with me, she rested a hand on her hip. "Is this about Russell?"

"Let's talk in the office."

I liked Paisley, and I liked Russell. They were both great at their jobs and great with everyone else on the team. Cade's observation might be on point.

A moment later, Paisley sat across from me, her shoulders tense and her jaw set. She didn't even give me a chance to start slow. "I don't know what the deal is, but Russell has an issue with me. I snapped at him, I admit it, but..." She shook her head slowly, releasing a puff of air that expertly got a loose lock of her auburn hair out of her eyes. "I'd think he had an issue with women as firefighters, but he doesn't behave that way around anyone other than me."

"Is there something I should know?" Maybe she'd be more open with me than Russell.

She shook her head before I could even finish asking. "Absolutely not."

"I hope this doesn't affect your work together."

"It definitely won't. I promise," Paisley assured me.

Maybe they hadn't acted on it, but I'd bet chemistry was sparking between them. I imagined myself attempting to work with Madison as a firefighter. The mere thought of it had me wanting to run. I'd be too worried about her. It simply wouldn't work. I knew it wasn't because she was a woman. I'd been on the town crew with Susannah for over two years. I trusted her completely, and she was an absolute badass in the field. I also knew Ward was prone to worrying about her, which was precisely why they weren't on the same crew together.

I left Paisley in my office and went to chase down Russell again. It only took thirty seconds in the small office with them together to realize they both had it bad. Paisley's cheeks flushed pink, and Russell cleared his throat uncomfortably.

I looked back and forth between them. "We're officially on call, so sort this out. All I expect is for you to be able to work well together. The rest, I don't care about."

With a nod, I closed the door behind me and left them in there alone. I trusted they could work it out. Russell was as solid as they came. I trusted Paisley, even if I hadn't known her as long as him.

Only one day after that, my crew got called out to a fire. Allie went to stay with my parents, and off we went. I experienced an unfamiliar moment as I was walking out to the helicopter that would take us to the backcountry. I wanted to text Madison and let her know I'd be gone, but it didn't feel quite right. The weekend we'd spent together had been enough to set the sheets on fire, but we weren't a couple. I was still trying to convince myself it was nothing more than some serious chemistry. But the urge to let her know I'd be gone for five days spoke volumes.

*She's just your neighbor.*

*That's not all she is to you.*

Fuck. I kicked that thought to the curb. If she

needed something, she might wonder where I was. Ah, I rationalized a reason to tell her. I slipped my phone out and zapped off a text.

Me: *Allie will be at my parents' for five days. I'm headed out to a fire in the backcountry. If you need anything, Janet's your best bet.*

I was sitting down in the back of the helicopter when I could feel my phone vibrate. Slipping it out, I glanced down to see her reply.

Madison: *Be safe.*

My heart thumped in reply.

"What are you smiling at?" Chase asked.

Whipping my head up, I shrugged. "Nothing."

*Bullshit.*

Any chance for conversation was drowned out as the helicopter started, the *thwack, thwack, thwack* of its blades filling the air.

I leaned my head back, picturing Madison—her dark hair tangled on the pillows.

## Chapter Twenty-Six

# MADISON

It was day three of Graham being gone, and I wanted an update. I loved updates. But I didn't think hotshot firefighting in the middle of the wilderness was the kind of job where updates were provided on the regular.

There was no reception where they were. I had tried, oh-so-casually, to gather information during my now daily stops at Firehouse Café. I was working, and I loved my job so far. Gratefully, that kept me busy, and it meant I didn't have to panic about money anymore, so I wasn't forced to ration my social trips to town.

My reconnaissance at the coffee shop had given me little nuggets of information. Graham was the superintendent of his crew, and they were fighting a fire that was a good hour away as the crow flew. Maisie knew everything because she was the main dispatcher. She was becoming what I thought might be a friend and had even mentioned we should get together one evening with some of her other friends. I was looking forward to it because Graham would be gone.

I felt silly over my small thrill at making friends. However, I was beyond grateful that I didn't have to wonder if they wanted to know me because of my family's connections. Those were tarnished, but it was nice not to wonder. Small favors and all that. I'd had another meeting with the attorney about my deposition, which was coming up next week. Fun stuff.

I was finishing up for work when my phone rang. I didn't get a ton of calls. When I looked down, I was surprised to see Allie's number flashing across the screen. Curiosity, of course, got the best of me, and I answered quickly.

"Hey, Allie, what's up?"

"I need some help, and you're probably going to think it's a bad idea." She sounded stressed.

"Tell me what's going on." Worry tightened in my chest. "Aren't you staying with your grandparents?"

"Yes, but I'm at school right now."

"Okaaaa-y," I said slowly, unease slithering down my spine. "Tell me what happened."

"I got caught smoking on school grounds," she said, her words coming out in a rush.

"And you're calling me about this?" My heart pinched with worry and empathy. Being a teenager wasn't much fun, and I still marveled that anyone pretended it was. Opportunities to make stupid and careless decisions abounded around every corner.

"I need someone to pick me up."

"Allie, I can't do that." I might've felt for her, but that answer was clear.

Allie burst into tears. "Please."

"Allie, I can't. I'm sure you only have a few people on your permission list, and I'm not one of those people."

"Actually, you are, because you picked me up that time."

*Oh, fuck, fuck, fuck.*

"Allie, I still can't do that, and I have to tell your father what happened."

Allie sniffled. "I don't want him to know."

"Look, I know it's not good to get caught smoking at school, but it's not the end of the world. I'm sure your dad will be reasonable about it when he gets back. Just tell your grandparents what happened, and you'll figure it out from there."

"Promise you won't tell my dad."

"Allie, I can't make that promise. What I will promise you is when he's back from wherever he is, I'll let him know we had this phone call."

Allie went quiet for a moment before she sniffled. "Fine. Thanks for nothing." Then she hung up.

I stared at the phone, uncertain what to do. I knew I couldn't pick her up. I wanted to call her grandparents, but I didn't know them very well, and I didn't have their phone number.

*Fuck, fuck, fuck.* This was not good. I really wished Graham were home. I couldn't keep this secret from him. With nothing to do to fix this, I started pacing back and forth in front of the windows. Wilbur sensed my upset and paced along with me. I reached down to stroke across his back just as my phone rang again. I raced over to my desk. This time, not recognizing the number, I answered with trepidation. "Hello?"

"Hi, is this Madison Glen?"

"Uh, yes."

"Hi, this is Ms. Smith, the vice principal at Willow Brook High School. Allie's grandparents aren't available to pick her up because they're in Anchorage for the next few hours. You're the only other person on the pickup list. Would it be possible for you to pick Allie up?"

I groaned silently. "Of course I can pick her up. I'll be there in twenty minutes."

I hung up, my unease multiplying inside. The second Allie climbed into my car, she set out to beg me not to tell her father why I had to pick her up early. While I had never been a mother, it only took me mere minutes to acquire an enormous amount of empathy for every parent of every teenager in the entire universe.

Wow, she was a master at putting the pressure on. I held firm and told her I wasn't going to lie on her behalf. When I pulled up in front of her grandparents' house, Allie's eyes beseeched me. "Please," she repeated for what must've been the hundredth time on the short drive.

I took a deep breath. "Allie, my answer is not going to change. I'm really sorry. I'm not comfortable keeping that secret."

She climbed out of the car, her shoulders hunched and her feet scuffing the ground as she walked up the stone walkway in front of the house. I left, feeling sad for her and nervous.

I decided to call Janet. She'd given me her phone number, and I figured I would at least tell her. Maybe she would know how to reach Allie's grandparents. Janet answered on the second ring. "Hi, Madison."

"How did you know it was me?" I was astonished.

"I have your number in my contacts. I had it before you even moved here. Your grandfather's attorney gave it to me."

"Oh, wow. That makes sense. I need your opinion." I quickly filled her in.

Janet replied matter-of-factly, "Of course you can't

keep that a secret, not that you're asking. I'll call her grandparents and let them know the school called you to give her a ride. It's that simple. I would let the rest of it go because it's not really your problem."

The tension in my shoulders eased as I let out a breath. "You're absolutely right. Thank you. You gave me permission to let it go, and I appreciate you calling them."

Janet chuckled, shifting gears so smoothly she caught me off guard. "How are things with you and Graham?"

"Um, what do you mean?"

I hadn't told a soul about what passed between Graham and me. There was *no* way Janet knew about our weekend together, or the other kiss, or that first kiss before I even knew I was going to be his neighbor.

"He's your closest neighbor. Plus, I think he likes you."

I almost choked. "What?" I squeaked.

Janet chuckled again. This time, I could hear the sly tinge in the sound. "I may be old, but I'm observant. That man could use a good woman in his life."

"I don't know what you're talking about," I replied, trying to sound all cool and collected when the feel of his hands mapping my body flashed through my thoughts. I was profoundly relieved she couldn't see how red my face was, considering it felt like it was on fire.

"I've got to run, new customers coming in." She hung up quickly as I said goodbye.

Allie getting caught smoking at high school really wasn't the end of the world. Not that I'd ever smoked in high school. I was ridiculously well-behaved. I still remembered the lecture I got from my then-boyfriend because I didn't have sex with him. I'd been home-coming queen and valedictorian of my class, and I'd never once felt I was cool, not for a second. Talk about appearances being deceiving.

After college, the outside of my life looked post-card-perfect—holiday cards to friends and family, and the like. And now, it felt like those pictures had been torn up, someone laughing as they tossed them in the air, the confetti singed by the fire of my father's betrayal. "Whatever," I muttered to myself.

The week passed, and I stayed busy with work, and there were no more calls from Allie. I *did* wonder how she was doing. I resisted the urge to text her and check in because I didn't feel like that was my role. I also wondered when I would see Graham again, and I wished I knew when he'd be back. I'd stopped with my casual questions at Firehouse Café because I'd give myself away if I got too nosy. I might not be an expert at small-town life, but I knew how gossip worked. It burned like a brush fire on the winds created by rumors. The smaller the community, the faster it burned with every little rumor setting new fires.

Everything was fine, even if I missed Graham more than was sensible. Well, everything was fine until that Saturday.

## Chapter Twenty-Seven

# GRAHAM

"What did you say?" I glanced at Allie where she sat beside me in the passenger seat of my truck. I had just turned the engine off in front of our house.

She looked down, twisting her fingers in her lap, a dead giveaway she was not telling me the whole story. "I said I got in trouble at school," she mumbled.

"Yeah, I got a message from the principal that you had to go home early one day. She didn't say why and told me to give her a call. Might as well tell me now."

Allie's eyes lifted, looking at me quickly before bouncing away again. "Have you talked to Madison?"

"Ah, no. I just got back this afternoon. Why would I have talked to Madison?"

"I thought maybe she told you."

"Told me what? I'm confused."

Allie blinked, dipping her head and mumbling something else.

"Allie, just tell me." When she stayed silent, I added, "I guess I'll call Madison since the school is closed, and I won't get the answer from them until Monday." I was wondering why Madison didn't call me, and I was getting angry. I didn't know where to direct it just yet.

"I got caught smoking," Allie blurted out, her voice rising sharply at the end. She stared at me with a hard, familiar, and stubborn look in her eyes.

"Smoking?"

"Yes, it's not a big deal. Madison said it wasn't that big of a deal."

"What?"

"That's what she said," Allie insisted. "The school had to call her because you put her on the list when she picked me up that day. Grandad and Gram were shopping in Anchorage."

"Do they know what happened?"

"Yes, they talked to the principal."

"Let's call Gram right now." I'd landed and gone straight to the school to pick Allie up.

I tapped the speakerphone and called. My mom answered, "Hi there, how was work?" she asked, as though she were asking about a regular workday.

I'd been gone for five days. I was exhausted and filthy and couldn't wait for a shower.

"Fine. Did you talk to the principal about Allie?" I asked, getting right to my point.

Allie gritted her teeth, and I could see a muscle tightening in her jaw. "I certainly did. It sounds like I'm on speaker."

"Allie's right here."

"They sent her home early after she got caught smoking. She had detention, and she's got to participate in an educational program at the school. She didn't get to see any friends after school. I planned to talk to you about it this evening. Did you tell him?" my mother asked, directing her question to Allie.

"Of course I did. Why do you think he's calling you?" she replied, her tone just barely polite.

"Good for you. Need anything else?" my mom asked calmly.

"Not at all. Thank you for handling it." I hung up and looked at my daughter. "Should I call Madison with you?"

Allie shook her head quickly, and I didn't have the heart to put her through that. I didn't want to put Allie on the spot in front of Madison, but I intended to have a conversation with her. It was not cool to tell Allie smoking was no big deal.

"Did you ever get caught smoking at school?" my daughter asked, her eyes flashing.

"That doesn't really matter."

"I'm just curious," she pressed.

I rolled my eyes. "Actually, no, I didn't." I wouldn't have won any awards for being a saint in high school, but I'd been more focused on girls and sports than smoking.

"Whatever." Allie swung away and flounced out of a car.

I wanted to drive straight over to Madison's. My shower was calling, but the urge to get this conversation over with was even stronger. I leaned out of the car, calling, "I'll be back in a few! I expect you to stay here."

"I know!" she called over her shoulder.

I put my truck in reverse, turning around quickly and driving the short distance from our place to Madison's. When I pulled up, she was standing at the back of her car with the door open and what looked to be bags of groceries on the back seat. She paused what she was doing, turning to look over at me. I was annoyed, really annoyed. I climbed out.

"Got a sec?"

She nodded, her eyes coasting over my face. That little bolt of heat that happened whenever I got near her sizzled through my body. I ignored it, focusing on my frustration.

"Thanks for picking Allie up when my parents were busy."

"No problem. Everything okay? I was planning to call you when you got back, but I didn't know when that would be."

"It's fine. I'm just wondering why you would have told Allie smoking at school is no big deal."

Madison stared at me for a long moment. "That comment in context makes more sense. She was crying, and I was trying to let her know it wouldn't be the end of the world."

That made complete sense, but I was still annoyed, and I didn't even know why. Maybe because I was tired. Maybe because I had a teenager who occasionally pushed my buttons. Maybe because I had the hots and then some for this gorgeous woman standing in front of me. She was a walking complication, and I didn't like it. All I said was, "Right. Of course it's not."

We stared at each other, and nothing about this felt right. "Well, thanks for clarifying."

"Of course."

Madison opened her mouth to say something else, but I didn't wait to listen. I turned and climbed back in my truck, managing to wave as I drove away. Inside, I knew I was overreacting. I knew I was pinning my frustration on Madison, but I didn't like how easily she distracted me.

When I returned home, Allie's bedroom door was firmly closed. I lifted my hand to knock but lowered it slowly. We'd already had our conversation, so there was nothing left to discuss.

After a quick shower, I snagged a beer out of the fridge and kicked my feet up on the coffee table, trying to distract myself by watching sports. My thoughts kept boomeranging back to Madison. I'd hated the look in her eyes. I was annoyed with my frustration and with myself. I wished the situation was different. Maybe it was for the best. We were worlds apart. My body didn't get the memo, though. I went to sleep restless and thinking of her. Too bad desire wasn't logical.

———

The following morning, I trudged into Firehouse Café for coffee. Snow dusted the ground, and I tapped it off my boots as I stepped through the door. I heard Madison's voice instantly. It rang like a bell in my awareness. Looking ahead, I saw her standing at the counter, gesturing with one hand as she talked to Janet. Janet was laughing and leaned over to lightly squeeze Madison's shoulder affectionately.

I took a breath and kept walking. Madison glanced my way. The second her eyes collided with mine, her smile faded swiftly, and tension lined her face. "Hi," she murmured, giving me a tight smile.

I nodded. "Hi, how's it going?"

"Fine." She stepped to the side.

Janet's eyes shifted from Madison to me, curiosity flickering in her gaze. I adored Janet, but she was definitely nosy. "What can I get for you?"

"My usual."

Janet turned to prep the coffee, and Madison called, "Nice to see you, Janet."

Janet waved, and I resisted the urge to look over my shoulder and watch Madison leave. It took more effort than I wanted to admit. When I turned to Janet, she looked at me skeptically.

"What's going on?" she asked.

"I'm getting coffee before I go into the station," I replied, hewing to the concrete.

Her eyes narrowed. "I mean, with Madison."

"Nothing, Janet," I finally said.

"I thought you liked her."

"I do. She's a nice girl."

"No, I thought you *really* liked her."

"Janet," I said, my tone a warning.

She shrugged lightly. "I heard about the cigarette thing."

"What about it?"

"Madison had to pick her up."

"What does this have to do with anything?" I countered, irritation prickling over my skin.

Janet passed me my coffee and rang me up. I took a long swallow, appreciating the bitter flavor because it suited my mood.

"Did Madison talk to you about that?" I asked.

"No, your mother did. She said she thought you were going to be upset with Madison about it."

"I'm not upset with Madison," I said quickly, too quickly.

Janet arched a brow. "I think you're looking for an excuse."

"An excuse for what?" I sputtered, unable to hide my frustration.

"You are an incredible father, and you have a lovely daughter. But she's like a shield for you. For what it's worth, I think you're a smart man. I don't think you've consciously avoided getting involved with anyone all this time, but you did need to focus on your daughter, and your job didn't make it easy. My gut tells me you might really like Madison, but you're so accustomed to doing things on your own that it kind of scares you to take someone else seriously. That's what I mean. You're looking for an excuse. That's all." She shrugged lightly as if she hadn't just blasted through all of my well-established defenses about myself and my life.

I had plenty to say, most of it hot air, but I was saved by a group of tourists tromping in through the door. "Think about what I said," Janet called as I turned to leave after giving her a big tip even though I was annoyed with her.

I simply waved and left. Once I got out to the parking lot, my eyes were drawn like a magnet to Madison. She was standing by her car with one hand curled around the door handle and the other on her phone. Her voice carried to me because my truck was on the other side of hers.

I'd been so distracted when I arrived I hadn't even noticed I parked beside her.

"Mom, I can't do that. You have to understand." Her voice sounded distressed. I saw her head nodding in response to whatever her mother said. She held still and began shaking her head. "No, I'm not moving back to Houston, and I'm not lying for Dad. It's not happening. I have to go."

She hung up, and I watched from behind as her shoulders rose with a deep breath and then fell abruptly. As if she sensed me, she turned around. Her cheeks went pink as she stared at me. Without a word, she spun away and climbed into her car.

I watched as she drove away, wondering just what the hell she was talking about. A short while later, I was at the station in the office, eyeing my laptop. Firefighters didn't need computers, or so I thought. As the superintendent for the crew, I had to schedule training and check in about budget stuff. Occasionally, I even had to check email.

I stood from my chair and then sat down again. Another moment later, I was searching Madison's name online. Lo and behold, there was a lot to be found. As my mother had already discovered, her father had been arrested for fraud. Madison was considered a primary witness against him. If I'd wondered if we were from different worlds, my little internet search verified it times a million. She came from money, serious money. There were pictures of her at society events in Houston looking absolutely stunning. I knew she had great legs, but seeing her in a fitted skirt that flared at her knees and wearing strappy heeled sandals, sweet Jesus. I didn't know what to think of any of this.

It broke my heart a little to see the various news stories about Madison. Some of them were just fluff, photos of her at society events and so on. Then her father got arrested. Clearly, he was part of Houston society. As the media was wont to do, they circled like vultures around her family, speculating on her refusal to testify and her tight-lipped silence about the case.

They even speculated on why her engagement ended within two weeks of the charges being filed. Her former fiancé, the fucking asshole, announced he had no idea what had been going on and that they'd grown apart. Whatever the fuck that meant. *Fuck you, asshole. You didn't grow apart.* Earlier reports indicated that her fiancé had aspired to benefit from her family connections. They said right in print that she was no longer a benefit to him. The speculation was that what she thought was a love match had never been.

"You fucking asshole," I muttered as I stared at the computer. Of course, the man had nothing to say in return.

I felt for her, but I also knew we weren't and could never be a couple. For real. Knowing that, why did my heart burn, almost stinging from the pain?

## Chapter Twenty-Eight

# MADISON

"You've got this," the prosecutor said firmly.

As we stared at each other over the video conference call, her gaze softened. "I know this isn't easy for you."

My throat was tight. "It's not, but thank you for understanding."

The prosecutor was quiet for another moment before cocking her head to the side and commenting, "I hope you have some support. It's hard to be a witness against a parent."

I nodded, swallowing through the tightness in my throat. It felt like a ball of disappointment, regret, and anger with pain tangling inside all of it. I'd never had an amazing relationship with my parents. Our family just wasn't like that.

I *had* been shocked when my parents expected me to commit crimes on their behalf or, rather, cover them up, which would've made me an accessory. I hadn't realized how much of my relationship with them relied on me toeing the line and doing what worked for them.

After a sip of my water, I replied, "It is hard, but I'm finding my way."

"How do you like Alaska?"

I managed a small smile. "Actually, I like it. My grandfather's home is beautiful. It's such a change of pace that it's been good for me."

"I bet it's beautiful there. Alaska makes Texas seem small."

I chuckled. "I suppose."

"I heard about your new job," she commented.

I narrowed my eyes. "How would you know that?"

She grinned. "We have to keep tabs on witnesses. No big deal. You're very good at your job, so I'm glad you've found work."

I was fiddling with a paperclip with one hand, and I paused. "Am I, though? Because I should've noticed what was going on."

"You worked with the numbers you had. Being good at your job doesn't mean knowing someone else was providing you with false information." She glanced at her watch. "I have another meeting in a few minutes. Your deposition went very well, and you handled the difficult questions from your father's attorney as well as could be expected."

"Do you think I'll need to testify?"

She tapped her fingertips on her desk. "I don't know. Your father has a good attorney, and a good attorney gives clients good advice. We have a really strong case. If his attorney's doing his job, he'll make your father understand that. It's a smart move to try to make a deal with us, but I sense that your father can be stubborn."

I laughed aloud at that. "Absolutely, but he's also not stupid. I don't think he'll enjoy being in jail for too long if he's facing any time."

She dipped her head in acknowledgment. "No, I can't imagine he would. I'll keep you posted when we have any updates. As you know, waiting for court can be like watching paint dry, so be patient."

"I will. Please keep me posted."

We ended the call, and I stared out the windows. Wilbur was asleep at my feet. I stood, heading to the kitchen to get some coffee. I was tired. I hadn't realized how much tension it would create to sit through that three-hour deposition.

After I started the coffee, I swung my arms in the air to try to loosen up my shoulders. My mind shifted to Graham. He had a dedicated channel, like a television station, in my brain. It tuned to him whenever I wasn't completely distracted. I felt unsettled about how things had played out. It wasn't as if we had defined what was going on with us.

I leaned my head back and let out a sigh, my throat tightening yet again. I had *really* started to fall for him. I hadn't expected it. I hadn't expected him *at all*.

Obviously, he didn't want anything serious. I could even understand why he'd taken my comment to Allie out of context, but I was still annoyed at his assumption.

I heard the sound of Wilbur's claws on the floor and turned to see him entering the kitchen. My dog remained my best friend, and my heart pinched at the longing I hadn't let myself truly feel for Graham. I'd wanted more and was so skittish about it.

I hoped this bout of tension would pass, and we could settle into being friendly neighbors. I hated how vulnerable I felt. I hated how much I missed Graham. And how could I even miss him? It wasn't like we'd had that much time together. I missed him even more than I'd ever missed my ex-fiancé, who'd been part of my life for years.

My treacherous heart skipped a beat, and my belly spun. All I had to do was think about my nights with Graham and his hands on my body. Those times with him were raw and pure—like nothing I'd ever experienced. The memories were branded into my brain and on my body, my cells recalling the visceral feel.

I poured my coffee and returned to my desk. My new job was working out well, and I'd also started doing some small accounting jobs on the side, including for the gallery business Janet had told me about. It felt so good to dive into numbers because they always made sense. I was starting to feel competent again, and I craved that feeling. When I was working, I could forget Graham and forget the simmering tension between my parents and me that I didn't know how to repair.

Late at night when I wasn't working and loneliness pierced me, I missed the glimmer of wondering if maybe Graham wanted more than sex with me. Hope was such a tease. Yet it wasn't rational, and it wasn't sensible. I shouldn't have hoped for more with Graham.

All mental lectures aside, I reached for my phone, my fingertips itching to text him. The only thing that stopped me was the time on the clock—midnight.

———

A week passed, and I was handling life. I worked. I stayed busy. I only went to get coffee three times that week. I was even invited to a girls' night at Wildlands. Maisie had run into me in the parking lot at Firehouse Café and invited me along.

That evening, I looked down at Wilbur after he finished eating his evening meal. "Okay, I'll be back in a few hours. I won't be too late."

Wilbur blinked up at me with his bottom wiggling. He wasn't used to me leaving, not since we'd moved here. I figured he would sleep. I was wearing a fitted pair of jeans with low-heeled boots and a silky blouse. I slipped into a lightweight down jacket. A short while later, I crossed the parking lot into the entrance at Wildlands, recalling my dinner here with Allie and Graham.

I'd seen her and Graham at Firehouse Café a few days ago, and we'd been polite. Allie had asked me when we could have a nail-painting party again. I couldn't help but wonder if Graham had given up on helping her dye her hair, which kind of made me sad. I shook my head, trying to kick those thoughts loose. Graham was practically living inside my brain, and I really needed to boot him out.

When I walked into the bar and glanced around, I saw Maisie waving from a table in the corner. She was seated with several other women, and I felt a little nervous.

"Hey!" Maisie called as I approached the table. "We saved a chair for you." She pointed at the one empty chair.

I rounded the table to sit down, shimmying out of my coat and hanging it over the back of the chair.

Maisie began pointing from one woman to the next. "This is Lucy. She's married to Levi. I don't know if you've met him yet. This is Amelia, and she's married to Cade. Lucy and Amelia have a construction business together. This is Susannah, she's married to Ward. Jasmine, is Levi's sister and is married to Dono- van. And this is Paisley. She's a new firefighter at the station." Her gaze arced around the table. "Everybody, this is Madison. She's Harold's granddaughter. Remember Harold? He used to come up here for half of the year."

Amelia glanced at me. "Oh, he's got a great house. We actually helped him update it when he bought it." Lucy was nodding along.

"You helped update his house?" I couldn't keep the surprise out of my tone.

Amelia cast me a quick smile. "We sure did." Amelia was tall and leggy, while Lucy was petite with a fairy-like quality to her.

I glanced between them. "Well, that's badass."

Lucy chuckled. "Our business is Kick-Ass Construction."

"Okay, it's kick-ass then."

"Paisley's even newer to town than you," Maisie offered.

"What do you think of Willow Brook so far?" I asked.

She smiled. "I like it. I'm settling in."

There was a lull in the conversation when the waitress arrived. After we ordered, Maisie turned to Paisley. "Is Russell still being an asshole?"

Paisley shook her head quickly. "Graham had a conversation with both of us. It hasn't been as tense since then. I want to say it's because I'm a woman, but he's not like that toward you." She gestured toward Susannah. "You're a firefighter too."

Susannah's strawberry blond curls bounced with her nod. She pursed her lips as she eyed Paisley. "I think Russell likes you."

Paisley rolled her eyes. "Bullshit."

"I happen to agree," Maisie chimed in.

"Is this how it's gonna be?" Paisley asked as she glanced around the table.

"How what's going to be?" Lucy returned politely.

"Everybody having an opinion," Paisley said bluntly.

"I think so. It's a small town," I offered dryly.

"We might be nosy, but we actually care. If Russell keeps being a dick, just say the word. I'll make sure he straightens out," Susannah offered with a wink.

Paisley grinned, and the conversation moved on. It was nice, really nice, to have dinner and just hang out. These women could not have cared less about my family's situation, and I loved that.

About halfway through dinner, I felt a prickle of awareness chase down my spine. I knew, I just *knew*, Graham had entered the restaurant.

Maisie, showing off her mind-reading capabilities, asked just then, "Is Graham being a good neighbor?"

"Sure," I said with a light shrug, hoping the heat flashing into my cheeks didn't show.

Jasmine cocked her head to the side, a smile teasing at the corners of her mouth. "Janet thinks Graham has a thing for you."

I rolled my eyes and took a swallow of my water. "He's definitely not interested. I don't think I'm the kind of girl he has in mind." Then my worries tumbled out. "Plus, he got upset with me."

I quickly summarized the situation, and Amelia shook her head. "That's not like Graham to overreact."

"I think he's overreacting for a reason," Susannah offered.

I looked at Paisley. "You're right. This is how it is."

She shrugged, and the conversation carried on. The group gradually began to filter out. Beck came to get

Maisie and pulled her close for a kiss. The moment was brief, but the look he gave her was so intense, I had to look away. Of course, my eyes landed on Graham. The dull ache of missing him was abruptly sharp.

His eyes held mine for a second, and I gave him a tight smile. I could do this. I could get used to this. It was nothing, just a little fling. I'd never regretted my lack of fling experience so much in my life.

I hurried away after that. I felt antsy and silly because, somehow, I doubted he missed me the way I missed him

## Chapter Twenty-Nine

# GRAHAM

"Why did you do that?" Allie asked, her chin set in a mulish line and her eyes flashing. We were at the kitchen table, and I hadn't had enough coffee yet.

"Do what?"

"Stop being friends with Madison."

"I'm still friends with Madison," I insisted.

Allie's curls bounced with the sharp shake of her head. "When we saw her at Firehouse, you were all polite and weird. I thought you actually liked her."

God save me from my way too perceptive daughter. "I do like her."

"You *like* her, like her?" my daughter pressed.

I bit back a groan. "I like her as a neighbor and a friend." I paused to take a gulp of coffee.

Allie blinked at me. "I think you're being stupid. Gram said you were upset because Madison told me it wasn't a big deal to get caught smoking. You took it out of context."

Fuck my life. Why did teenagers have to be so pushy? "You're right. I did take it out of context. Madison explained, and I'm not upset."

Allie sighed. "Why do you use me as an excuse?" she asked next.

"What are you talking about?" I muttered, dipping my head and taking a deep breath. We'd already covered this topic, but here we were again. I slid my hand through my hair as I straightened.

"You never date, and I'm your excuse."

"You're not an excuse, Allie. You're a priority."

She wrinkled her nose. "I don't think so. I want you to go apologize to Madison about your weird attitude."

I almost burst out laughing because she was talking to me like I was a bratty kid. I blinked at her. "Allie, this isn't your issue."

"It is. I want to be friends with her."

"You *are* friends with her."

"Yeah, but it's weird if you're weird about her."

This conversation was going in circles, but pointing that out wouldn't change it. So, I said, "If you want to go spend time with Madison, just let me know when you'll be back."

Allie stood from the table. "You're avoiding my point," she said pointedly, complete with her index finger pointed right at me.

"Lots of pointing," I observed.

She rolled her eyes and went to put her cereal bowl in the sink before flouncing out of the room and going into her bedroom. It was Saturday, and it had been two full weeks since my weekend with Madison.

My daughter might be right, and that was uncomfortable. Even more uncomfortable was how much I missed Madison. I missed her so much my heart ached. I missed her so much I'd looked at those online photos of her more than I wanted to admit, just because she was so beautiful. I shook my head and took a deep breath. This would pass. It had to.

My thoughts were taken off of Madison when my phone rang. Glancing at the screen. I saw Allie's mother's number flashing. Great, fucking great. Not who I wanted to talk to now, but I might as well get it over with. I swiped my thumb across the screen.

"Hi, Alison. What's up?"

"I was thinking of scheduling another visit," she said easily.

I was already cranky. Her entitlement rankled me. "I really don't want you to talk to Allie about it until you're actually here."

"Graham, that's not fair," she said, sounding all affronted.

I couldn't find a single fuck to give for her feelings. "You've let Allie down more than once. I can't trust you to be reliable," I said flatly.

Just then, Allie appeared in the kitchen as if she had a radar and knew that her mom was on the phone. Crossing her arms, she leaned her shoulder against the archway into the kitchen.

Meanwhile, her mother said, "You're being ridiculous."

I took a breath, letting it out slowly. "No, I'm not. Just let me know when you're planning for, and we'll figure it out from there." I hung up before she could say anything else.

Allie glared at me, her eyes glistening with tears. "That was Mom, wasn't it?"

"It was." I'd promised myself to always be honest about these things.

"Is she coming to visit?"

"She said she'd like to plan another trip. I told her to confirm when she was actually here."

I braced myself because I'd long ago learned that I was the one who absorbed my daughter's anger at her mother.

Allie blinked and lifted her chin. "I'm old enough to handle it if she cancels."

"I know you are, hon."

I approached her because I wanted to hug her, but she was having none of it. She was the teenage equivalent of a cactus. She blinked rapidly and took a step back, shaking her head. "It's okay, Dad."

She spun around and dashed down the hall, slamming her bedroom door loudly. I was grateful she had a sturdy door. Taking a breath, I let it out in a sigh and turned to slump into a chair by the kitchen table. Nothing could prepare me for how much I wanted to make everything okay for my child. I wanted to wrap her in bubble wrap, but I couldn't.

Allie ended up leaving for the day to go to a friend's house. I thought that was for the best. She needed breathing room from me, and I could use a break from her prickly silent treatment.

I was outside chopping wood later that afternoon when I heard a piercing bark. Glancing up, I saw Wilbur coming through the trees from Madison's property.

This was strange. He'd never once come over here, and I knew she didn't let him wander. When he reached me, I knelt to pet him. As soon as I straightened, he barked again, looking toward the path between our properties.

"What's up?" I asked conversationally.

He answered with another bark. I set the ax down and snagged my jacket from where it rested on the woodpile. Shrugging into it, I tugged off my leather gloves. I decided to follow him over to her place. I told myself it was nothing.

I couldn't shake the unease slithering down my spine, though. We passed the entrance to the hunting trail that led into the valley. Wilbur stopped there and barked several times. I kept walking to Madison's place. I was finally thinking of it as hers, instead of her grandfather's.

My heart twisted sharply at that. I'd felt this echoing ache for two full weeks, missing her and missing the anticipation of maybe seeing her again.

I'd created a chasm between us, and I didn't know how to cross it. We got to her house, but there was no sign of Madison. Her door was unlocked, and when I walked in, nothing but an echoing silence greeted me. Wilbur didn't even come into the house. He stood by the door and barked.

"Bud, I wish you could tell me where she was."

He trotted down the steps, glancing over his shoulder and waiting. "Okay," I said. "Take me to her."

My unease had shifted into full-blown worry. I patted my jacket pocket to make sure I had my cell phone, then Wilbur and I set out. I followed as he turned up the hunting trail I'd pointed out to her a few weeks ago. He trotted along at a good clip for such short legs.

We'd gone about two miles when Wilbur stopped by an opening in the trees. The view offered a nice panorama of the valley and the mountain ridge on the far side.

He barked again, and I stared down at him. "Wilbur, I don't know where she is."

He startled me when he darted off the trail and began to make his way down into the valley. None of this made sense, but at this point, Wilbur was my only guide. I elected to follow him and promptly discovered he was far more nimble than me. He dashed around boulders and ducked under the brush with ease.

Just as I was starting to think we needed to turn back because this wasn't going to work, he barked again. Looking ahead, I saw him perched on a boulder. I followed his gaze to see a flash of bright blue. It was the same blue as the down jacket I'd seen Madison wearing the other day at the café. She must've veered off the main trail.

Distracted, I took a step and slipped, one of my feet catching on the thick underbrush. My elbow struck a boulder as my feet gave out. I let out a sharp grunt of pain. Wilbur glanced back, trotted to me, and nipped at my knee impatiently.

The reverberating nerve pain radiated from my elbow up to my shoulder as I shook my arm. I took the moment to glance around and then clambered to my feet again. "All right, bud, get me to Madison."

I didn't think this route was how Madison had gotten to where she was, but Wilbur had settled on a shortcut. I cupped my hands around my mouth, calling, "Madison!"

A moment later, I heard her voice in return. "Over here! Is that you, Graham?"

Relief rushed through me. "It's me. Wilbur found a shortcut. Are you okay?"

"Yes!" she called in return.

Wilbur picked up his speed at the sound of her voice. He ducked under a fallen tree while I had to climb over it. I kept my eyes on that patch of royal blue. As we got closer, I could make out her shape and realized she was sitting on a small boulder partially obscured by trees. I didn't know how long it took us to get to her, maybe another ten minutes, but it felt like forever.

When Wilbur got to her side, he leaped onto the boulder, nuzzling into her and licking her face. I pushed through the tree branches, my heart pounding in an unsteady, reckless beat. A mix of worry and relief rushed through me.

"Are you sure you're okay?" I asked when I finally reached her.

Madison looked a little dazed as she stared at me, and she was shivering. "What the hell happened?" I asked when I stopped beside her. My heart felt squeezed tight.

I quickly shrugged out of my jacket and wrapped it around her shoulders. She blinked at me. "I don't know. I fell."

I quickly brushed her hair to the side, my gaze traveling over her scraped cheek. There was a thin trail of dried blood right inside her hairline. "You must've hit your head." Panic struck me, but I forced myself to focus.

"How many fingers am I holding up?"

Madison obediently counted out three. I ran through several more tests to assess her basic mental function. "If you have a concussion, it's mild. I'm guessing you knocked yourself out, so Wilbur came to find me."

My eyes scanned the area, following along the steep incline directly above. "Do you remember falling?"

She nodded. "I slipped on some damp leaves up there. I don't know where my phone is. When I came to, Wilbur was gone."

She was still shaking. I knew the quickest thing to do was to get her back home. Even if I called for help, we could be home by the time they got here.

"Can you walk?"

Her head bobbed up and down quickly. "I walked around calling for Wilbur already."

I eyed the cliff before looking back at Madison again. "Let's go. We'll take the shortcut. I'm worried you're almost hypothermic."

"I'm fine, just a little cold," she insisted, although her teeth were chattering.

We were at a high enough elevation that frost had created patches of ice in the shade.

"Wilbur took off. It's only been a half an hour or so, and I was just waiting."

"Why didn't you call?" I asked, guilt tangling into my worry. I knew I'd deliberately kept my distance from her.

"I just told you I lost my phone. It fell out of my pocket. I was going to start walking again and figure it out, but I was worried about where Wilbur went."

"I'll call your phone. I'm sure we can find it." My eyes scanned the area again, lingering on the steep and rocky incline where she'd slipped down. When my gaze arced to her, I asked, "What happened to your face?"

"When I fell, I must've scraped it on some branches on the way down," she muttered.

As soon as I dialed her phone, a song broke out. Specifically, Linda Ronstadt's "You're No Good." I gave her a quizzical look.

"That's your new song," she said pertly.

I was torn between being affronted and relieved she felt good enough to have an attitude. I simply shook my head, listening for the song as I walked around at the base of the hill. After another call, I fished it out of the leaves and brought it to her.

"You ready to go?"

She nodded. "I don't think we can get up there."

I eyed the hill. "Probably not. We'll take Wilbur's shortcut. He's faster than us, but it works."

When Madison stood, and I looked down at her, I wanted to hold her, so I did. Stepping closer, I smoothed her tangled hair away from her eyes. Lightly brushing my knuckles over her scraped cheek, I asked, "Does it hurt?"

"A little. It stings more than anything," she replied as she looked up at me.

"I missed you."

My words surprised me. Not because I didn't mean them or feel them deeply, but because I wasn't prone to expressing myself.

"I thought you were mad at me," she whispered.

I shook my head. "I was mad at myself."

"For what?"

Wilbur barked, breaking into our conversation. I smiled down at him. "Let's get you home, and then we'll talk." He barked again, clearly impatient with us. I cast a rueful smile at her. "I think Wilbur wants to go."

"Ya think?" she teased lightly.

Madison was mostly fine, I hoped, but I felt a mess inside. My heart had tripped and fallen and was skidding sideways. I didn't know how this was even possible, but I loved Madison.

She'd slipped through my defenses like a thin ribbon of air around the edge of a window. I didn't even think she'd tried. Yet here she was—this beautiful, out of her element woman and former homecoming queen—giving me a slightly impatient look as she stared up at me. I wanted to tell her how I felt right this second, but I didn't even know if I was ready, much less her.

When Wilbur barked again. I reached for her hand. We made our way back to the main path by following Wilbur. Despite pushing branches out of the way and climbing over a few boulders, I managed to keep a hold of her hand every step of the way.

When we reached the main trail, Wilbur's step was almost jaunty now. He kept glancing back toward Madison and then circling our ankles. At one point, my eyes slid sideways to Madison's, and I asked, "Corgis are herding dogs, right?"

She nodded and let out a soft laugh. The sound spun around my heart like a lasso cinching. When we reached the juncture where the trail intersected with the path between our houses, I looked down at her.

Graham stared at me, his eyes searching mine. All the while, my heart felt like a bird trapped in a cage and trying to escape. He was looking at me like I was fragile and I might break at any minute. I didn't even know what to think that somehow Wilbur had found him and brought him to me. I would've made my way home. I knew exactly where I was. It was just when Wilbur took off and hadn't come back right away, I'd gotten worried.

Without a word, he turned and kept a hold of my hand, practically pulling me along the path toward my place.

"Do you need to let Allie know where you are?" I asked.

"She's at a friend's house," he replied curtly.

Although I was still cold and feeling a little numb, Graham's jacket did help. He seemed completely unaffected by the cold. Moments later, he had me in the house and was yanking me down the hallway to my bedroom.

"What are you doing?" I asked. Wilbur trotted along at my side.

"We need to get you in the shower and get you warmed up."

"I'm fine. My teeth aren't chattering anymore."

Graham narrowed his eyes. "Shower. I'm calling the EMTs to come out and check on you. Actually, you know what?" he asked himself apparently. "I'll just call Charlie. She lives nearby."

"Who's Charlie?" I asked. He was yanking my jacket off.

"Graham," I said sharply.

His head whipped up, his phone in hand. "I'm fine. I am cold, but I'm fine."

We stared at each other quietly, and I could hear every beat of my heart. He took a breath, closing his eyes and then opening them as he let it out slowly. "I still want you in that shower. It'll warm you up."

"Okay," I said softly. Realizing he was going to insist and feeling unsettled inside, I blurted out my question. "Do you think I'm a flake and not the kind of girl you could be with?"

Graham's eyes searched mine. The look he held there was so intent my breath seized. "Never," he whispered.

He dipped his head and stepped close, folding me into his arms. When he brushed his lips over mine, a tingling sensation chased from the point of contact and radiated through my entire system.

It felt so decadently good to be in his arms. When he lifted his head, his words shocked me. "I missed you."

I stared up at him. "I thought you were mad at me." He shook his head quickly.

"No, I was annoyed with myself."

"You think we're *not* right together, don't you, though?"

"No, that's not it."

"But I was homecoming queen, just like Allie's mom."

"You're nothing like Allie's mom," he said, his tone low.

"How do you know? Plus, I'm a city girl. I'm only here because I lost my job when my dad got arrested for fraud."

"I don't care if you're a city girl, and I definitely don't give a shit what your dad did. You're tough, you're smart, and you have a big heart." He brushed my hair away from my face. "I know we need to have this conversation, but first, you need to get in the shower. You're still cold."

His hands slid down my arms, curling around mine, and I could feel the contrast of his warm palms to my clammy hands. "Okay, I'll shower," I agreed.

"I'm gonna call Charlie. She lives about a quarter mile away."

"Who is Charlie?" I repeated.

"She's a local doctor. I just want to make sure you're okay, so I'd like someone to check you out."

I rolled my eyes. "Fine. Now go." I waved out the bathroom doorway. "I'd like to shower in peace."

He stepped out of the bathroom, and I closed the door behind him. "I'm right here if you need anything," he called through the door.

"I know!"

My belly felt funny, and my heart was pounding madly. The shower *did* feel really good. While I thought I'd have found my way back on my own, warmth curled around my heart at the thought that Graham had come to find me. After I finished showering, I dried off and dressed in my most comfortable clothes—a pair of fleece sweatpants and a fluffy sweater. I could hear voices as I padded down the hallway.

When I walked into the kitchen, a woman turned and smiled. Her dark hair was up in a ponytail, and she wore purple glasses that matched the bright streak of purple in her hair. "You must be Madison." She held her hand out as I approached.

I nodded, shaking her hand. "I am. Are you the doctor? You really didn't have to come. I think I'm fine."

"Charlie Franklin, nice to meet you. Graham said you would say you were fine. I'm sure you are, but he's worried. I live only a few minutes down the road. Let me just check on a few things."

She ran through the same concussion tests Graham had done, checked my eyes, and took a look at the scrape on my cheek and the cut by my hairline. "Everything looks fine. You'll be a little sore, but some ibuprofen should do the trick."

I glanced over at Graham. "I told you I was fine."

He shrugged, staring at me implacably. "You were unconscious long enough that Wilbur came to get me."

Charlie smiled down at Wilbur, who was sitting by her feet. "Wilbur is a good dog."

"The very best," I said.

"I should get going. Speaking of dogs, I need to feed ours, and Jesse's bringing home pizza for dinner."

"Do you know if he's picked it up yet?" Graham asked.

"I don't think so," Charlie replied.

"Think he'll mind if I ask him to get some for us?"

She smiled and shook her head.

"I could go get some," I offered.

"Nope, you shouldn't be driving, and I don't want to leave you alone," Graham said.

Charlie's eyes slid to mine, glinting with mirth. "Just call Jesse. I'm sure he'll pick up whatever you need and even deliver it for you. Please tip him, though," she teased.

I laughed softly. "Am I allowed to have spiked hot chocolate?" I asked Charlie.

She shook her head slightly. "I'd say not this evening. Head injuries can be unpredictable. You seem fine but wait until tomorrow. Somebody should check on you during the night."

"How often?" I asked, knowing this meant Graham would be staying here.

"Every four hours."

I sighed. Charlie left, and Graham called Jesse, ordering us two pepperoni pizzas. When he hung up, I asked, "Is Allie spending the night with her friend?"

"Oh, I need to call her too." Moments later, after he hung up, he said, "Yes, she is."

I rolled my eyes. Not much later, there was a sharp knock on the door followed by the sound of the door opening. The man I presumed to be Jesse appeared in the archway into the kitchen. "You must be Madison," he said with an easy smile. He had brown curls, a lighter shade than Graham's, and flashing green eyes.

"I am. You must be Jesse. Nice to meet you."

"Same. I'm delivering pizza." He held the box up in the air.

Graham grinned. "Let me get my wallet."

Jesse set the pizza on the table with a chuckle. "Consider it on me."

"Charlie said I had to tip you," Graham offered with a sly grin.

Jesse waggled his eyebrows. "Did she now? How much?"

I offered, "I would give a regular delivery driver maybe ten bucks."

"Ten bucks?" Jesse countered, his eyes widening.

"She's from Houston," Graham interjected, his tone deadpan.

I moved to stand from where I was sitting at the table, and Graham stepped swiftly to my side, placing a hand on my shoulder. "You don't need to get up." I rolled my eyes and met Jesse's bemused gaze as he looked from me to Graham and back again. "I slipped on some leaves and hit my head on a rock. Apparently, Graham thinks I can't even stand anymore," I offered dryly.

Jesse shrugged. "Well then, enjoy the pizza."

"I'll walk you out," Graham said.

I watched as they departed the kitchen and promptly stood and crossed over to the cabinet to get a glass and fill it with water. I got one for Graham while I was at it. "Actually, I should get him a beer," I said to myself, opening the fridge and fetching one for him. I also got two plates.

When he returned a moment later, I was back at the table. His eyes landed immediately on my glass of water, the beer, and the plates. "You weren't supposed to get up," he said.

"Graham, I walked all the way back with you. Obviously, I can stand. I'm fine. I'm totally fine."

"You were unconscious."

"I know, but I'm still fine," I insisted.

He muttered something under his breath and grabbed the beer off the table, returning it to the fridge. "Hey, I got that out for you," I protested.

"I don't need a beer," he said flatly as he sat down

across from me.

I opened the pizza box, and asked, "How many slices?"

He opened his mouth, and I held up a finger. "Don't you dare tell me I can't open the pizza box and get you some pizza." I pushed it to the middle of the table. "Pick your own," I muttered.

We ate quietly for a few minutes. After I finished off two slices of pizza, I leaned back in my chair, resting my hand on the table and watching Graham. He was terribly easy on the eyes. He was focused on his food and finished off a third slice before he even looked over at me. "What?" he prompted.

"Nothing."

"You're looking at me."

"Uh, you're sitting across from me." I snorted a little and took a swallow of water. I suddenly got nervous. "Look..." I began.

Graham started to reach for another slice of pizza, then he lowered it, fixing his gaze on me. "What is it?"

"I just thought I should tell you something."

"Okay."

"I thought maybe I should tell you how I ended up coming to Alaska. I was close to my grandfather, but he and my mother hardly ever spoke. I didn't even know he left me this place right away. Long story short, I worked for my family for years doing math."

"Doing math?" Graham asked, his eyes crinkling at the corners. One side of his mouth kicked up in a lopsided grin.

"Analyzing numbers is what actuaries do. Anyway, it turns out my father was committing financial fraud. I wasn't a part of it. He's facing charges and I'm testifying against him. My mother's furious at me, and I kind of lost everything. Fortunately, I had a little bit of my own savings, which floated me for a while. When I found out I'd inherited this place, I decided I might as well come here. I had nothing keeping me in Houston. I also learned the hard way that my fiancé didn't really love me, and my friends weren't the kind of friends who stick around when things go wrong."

I felt the burn of shame in my throat. When I lifted my eyes to find Graham's gaze waiting, there was no judgment, simply a calm, steady understanding.

"Honestly, when I first came here, I didn't know what I was going to do. I actually like it here, and I wasn't sure I would."

He nodded slowly. "Since we're being honest, you should know that I looked you up, so I knew that whole story. I didn't know how you felt about it."

My face burned. "You looked me up?" I whispered.

"Hey, don't stress." He reached over and put one of his big hands over mine.

His touch was warm and reassuring. "I was curious because I missed you. When I heard you on the phone in the parking lot with your mom, I got kinda nosy."

"Nosy? You?" I was honestly shocked.

Graham chuckled. "I'm not usually, but I guess I am about you. It's not your fault what your father did."

I shrugged. "I know, but I feel like I should have known."

"How are you supposed to know when somebody's doing something like that behind your back?"

I felt tears stinging in my eyes, and oh, my God, I did not want to cry in front of Graham.

As we looked at each other, my throat felt thick, and my chest hurt a little. All because of the look in his eyes. Like he actually believed in me.

In another second, he stood from the table and rounded to my side. Before I realized what was happening, he lifted me in his arms—without much trouble because he was that kind of man—and carried me into the living room.

I squeaked at the unexpected motion. "Where are we going?"

He sat down on the couch. It was then I realized he had started a fire while I was in the shower. He pulled me close to his chest. Graham had a great lap. He held me easily, his fingers sliding through the ends of my hair.

"If you need to cry, you can," he said, his voice rumbly and deep.

I blinked and took a breath. "I'm okay. My life kind of blew up, and I didn't even know who I was anymore."

"What do you mean?"

I pondered that, trying to collect my thoughts. "I don't know," I finally said. "I guess, having it all fall apart and realizing I didn't have anyone to turn to made me feel like my whole life, me included, was shallow and superficial. Like me being homecoming queen. That was a fluke too."

Graham's gaze was warm as he looked at me. I bit my lip.

"Yeah?" he prompted.

"It felt that way to me. When I came here, it was nothing more than a place to go. Now, I actually like my job, and this is a great little house."

His eyes arced about the space before coming back to mine. "It is. I think you're pretty awesome." His voice was all gravelly, and it did funny things to my insides as I stared into his eyes.

"You do?"

"You didn't notice?"

His fingers shifted up, and I felt the subtle brush

of his thumb along my collarbone. I tried to take a breath, but there didn't seem to be much air available. My stomach felt as if I were falling, and my pulse raced out of control like a horse set loose after being pinned up for too long.

"I thought I really screwed up with Allie."

Graham took a breath, his gaze sobering. "You didn't. I'm just not very good at parenting a teenager."

"That is not true," I said stoutly. "You're an incredible father to her. It's just that teenagers are kind of hard, I think. I've never had one, but that's my best guess."

His smile unfurled slowly across his face. My belly shimmied, and my skin felt like it was on fire under the path of his thumb tracing over my collarbone.

"I think you might be right. I'm the only parent who disciplines her, so sometimes she gets a little cranky with me. I'm learning it's part of the deal."

"It'll be okay," I offered.

"I know it will."

We looked at each other for a long moment, and then he shocked the hell out of me.

"I love you."

I must've stared at him for several beats too long because he prompted, "Madison?"

I took in a gulp of air. "What?" I squeaked.

His hand stilled before he brushed my drying hair away from my cheek. He dipped his head, pressing hot kisses along the underside of my jaw. When he lifted his head again, he spoke each word clearly, "I love you."

I felt a rushing sensation inside as if a wind was gusting through me, catching my heart and lifting it high. I was tingling all over, and all I could do was stare at him.

## Chapter Thirty-One

# GRAHAM

Madison's eyes were wide, and her mouth fell open in a pretty O. I sifted my fingers through her hair and waited. It felt beyond good to have her in my lap.

I didn't even want to think about how terrifying it had been to realize she could have gotten hypothermia. Hypothermia didn't seem like a big deal, but people died from it, most often during the autumn and spring seasons when they weren't as prepared for the cold. My brain slammed a door at the thought.

She was here, and she was safe. She was *mine*. She gave her head a tiny shake and then licked her lips. "You love me?"

I nodded slowly, certainty filling my heart and a sense of relief and joy settling inside me. "Yes. Is that so hard to believe?"

She blinked, and a tear rolled down her cheek. "Oh, don't cry. I don't handle tears well," I muttered as I brushed the tears off her cheeks with my thumb.

Her lips curled in a wobbly smile. "You have a teenage daughter," she pointed out. "Those hormones can make for some emotional times." I laughed and dipped my head to kiss her. When I drew back, I said, "It's okay if you're not there with me yet."

"I'm there. If you mean love, that is," she added quickly.

I heard myself repeating her question. "Are you sure?"

She pursed her lips, and I saw a glimpse of that prissy girl I'd met on the side of the highway. "Of course I'm sure. I don't say things like that lightly."

"I wasn't implying that." Pausing, I took in a deep breath. "I missed you like crazy."

"I thought I'd really upset you with that whole thing with Allie."

"It wasn't even that."

Madison's eyes searched mine. "What was it?"

She'd been honest with me, and now I had to be honest with her. Fuck. I took a breath. She reached for one of my hands, lacing her fingers through mine and resting it on her knee. That little point of contact was a touchstone for me.

"Allie got upset with me and said I was using her as an excuse."

"She did?"

I chuckled. "Yeah. My mom basically accused me of the same thing."

"Oh, I didn't even think your mom liked me."

"My mom can be protective. After what happened with Allie's mom, she's always been like that. But she liked you from the start. She was just trying to give me space to figure it out."

"What happened with Allie's mom?"

"I was young, and she was pretty."

"Did you think I was like her?"

I shook my head quickly. "Let me explain. She got pregnant. We didn't plan on it, obviously. A month after Allie was born, she took off. Since then, it's been Allie and me. Honestly, I did not have time for romance when Allie was younger. I don't know how anybody does. I also wasn't looking for it. Maybe I was skeptical about most women. Then you came along."

My heart thudded hard, and I felt exposed in a way I never had before as I looked into Madison's eyes. I took a steadying breath and forged ahead. "At first, I told myself it was just chemistry."

"We do have some pretty good chemistry," Madison offered, so earnestly I couldn't help but chuckle. Her cheeks went pink, and she shrugged. "Since we're being honest."

I sifted my fingers through her hair. "Sweetheart, it's more than pretty good. It's so good it freaked me out. When that thing happened with Allie, I really wasn't all that upset with you. I was upset with myself and not ready to face the fact that you had started to mean a lot to me. I also didn't know what you wanted."

Madison took a shaky breath before squaring her shoulders. Her lashes lifted, and her big green eyes met mine. "I didn't know what I wanted at first. I was kind of out of my element, so to speak. But now, I like it here. I'm even making friends."

"Of course you are. You're a good friend."

"You think?"

I nodded, my lips tugging into a grin. "You think you're gonna stay in Willow Brook?"

Madison stared at me for just long enough until uncertainty tightened inside me. Even if I was coming to terms with my feelings about her, Allie was my first priority. If Madison wasn't staying in Willow Brook. I couldn't even consider more with her. My life was way too busy to manage any kind of long-distance relationship.

Just when I was about to prompt again, she said, "Of course I am. For the first time in my life, I feel like I'm figuring out who I am, without all the props."

"Props?" I pressed.

She gave me a sheepish smile. "My family's business. My parents' money parlaying those connections into friendships that turned out to mean nothing when it mattered. Here in Willow Brook, it's just me."

We stared at each other for a moment, and it felt as if sparks filled the air around us. "I suppose, if we're not going to keep us a secret, I should ask about how you want to handle Allie."

"Let's talk about that later," I murmured. "Seeing as she's been on my case to date you, I don't think we need to worry."

"I know, but—"

I shook my head. "Enough talking. I missed you."

I dipped my head and blazed a trail of hot, open-mouthed kisses along the side of her neck and nipped at her earlobe. She shivered in my arms and let out a breathy whimper. Palming her cheek when I lifted my head, I stared into her eyes. I took a moment to simply absorb this woman. She was so strong and vulnerable at once.

"Mine," I whispered, my lips hovering above hers when I spoke.

Madison blinked, her lips moving against mine as she shifted incrementally closer. "No, you're mine."

We dived into a kiss, and I lost myself in her.

*Chapter Thirty-Two*

# MADISON

Almost a month had passed since Graham and I came to an agreement of sorts. We'd finally given in to the shimmer of passion and the emotion twined within it. As tempting as it was to spend every night together, we didn't. It was important to both of us that we move slowly for Allie's sake. She didn't need to feel as if we were rushing into things.

She knew we were dating, and I suspected she knew we stayed over together when she spent the night with friends. Graham teased that he thought she was going out of her way to give us time together.

My belly felt all fluttery when I rode home with him one evening. I was going to stay at his place, and Allie would be there. She knew I'd be there, but it didn't change how nervous I was. I smoothed my hands on my jeans.

"Are you sure this is okay?" I glanced over at him.

Graham was driving and kept his eyes on the road. It was snowing, my first big snowstorm. There had been a few dustings of snow so far, but apparently, we were predicted to get over a foot tonight. Wilbur was in the back seat of Graham's truck, his nose pressed to the window as he looked out into the swirling white flakes.

"Of course it's okay. I think it's time," Graham replied easily without even a hint of anxiety in his tone.

I took a breath, willing my nerves to settle. They were dancing along with uncertain anticipation. This felt monumental because committing to Graham meant committing to Allie. While I had no doubts about how I felt, I still didn't know how she really felt about her dad getting serious with someone.

A few minutes later, we came to a stop in his driveway, and I looked over at him. He turned the engine off, his eyes catching mine when he glanced sideways. "You don't need to be nervous."

My nerves weren't listening as I took an anxious breath. "Are you sure?"

He unbuckled his seat belt, angling to face me. He caught both of my hands in his when I turned toward him. "I'm absolutely sure. I love you."

It didn't seem to matter how often he said that. It was still a surprise. "I love you too, but what if—"

He shook his head. Releasing one of my hands, he placed his finger over my lips. "Allie will be fine. She really likes you. It's not like she doesn't know what's going on."

"What about her mother, though?"

Sadness chased through his eyes briefly. "She never did schedule that other trip she called about. It'll be okay. If Allie's going to be mad at anybody about her mother, it'll be me. Now, come on."

Moments later, we were in the kitchen. I had brought Wilbur's supplies, including one of his dog beds and some toys with us. I filled his water bowl and set it on the floor by the counter. Allie had been in her bedroom when we arrived, but she came down the hall, stopping in the entrance to the kitchen.

She held up a small box. "Will you help?"

I looked over. "With what?"

"Dyeing my hair. Dad failed."

Graham chuckled. "Oh yeah, you missed that. I tried, and it didn't go very well."

I laughed softly as I crossed over to Allie. "Do you want to do this before or after dinner?"

"What are we having for dinner?" she asked.

"I'm making spaghetti."

Allie grinned. "Ooh, that's his only specialty. You know that, right?"

A fizzy sense of joy rose inside with my laugh. "So I've heard."

After we had dinner, I helped Allie dye her hair. While we were waiting in the bathroom for the color to set, she looked over at me. I was perched on the edge of the tub, and she was sitting on the closed toilet.

"Dad really loves you," she said.

I felt a fluttery anxiety inside, but I tried to project a sense of calm. "How do you feel about that?"

"I like you, and I think it'll be okay." She held my gaze for a long moment, her lips curling into a slow smile. "This isn't why I like you, but it's really great to have somebody help me dye my hair without screwing it up."

I laughed, and she leaned over and gave me a quick hug. A little later, I asked, "What exactly happened when your dad tried to help? It's not that complicated."

Allie rolled her eyes. "He ended up panicking and

only let me do, like, two pieces. He also wouldn't let me keep it on long enough, so it just didn't work."

Our eyes met in the mirror, and we burst out laughing together.

Arms akimbo with my fists planted on my hips, I tilted my head back, looking up. "Are you sure this is okay?"

Graham called down. "Of course it's okay."

Graham—"my firefighter" as I'd come to call him —was high in a tree fetching the kitten we'd gotten for Allie. She was at school, and the kitten had escaped. I had to call him to come home.

Another voice reached me. "He'll be fine," Beck offered.

I glanced over at him. "Easy for you to say when you're not the one up in the tree."

Beck flashed an easy grin. I'd learned he'd once been known as the town's most shameless flirt. He was such a dedicated family man that it was hard to imagine, but I saw flashes of it.

He shook the rope in his hand. "I've got him."

"How does that even work?" I asked, dropping my arms and walking closer to Beck.

He quickly explained how rappelling worked to

me. "I promise, if he falls, I'll just catch him on the rope. It won't break."

"When I called you all, I thought you were going to bring the truck with the bucket and everything."

Beck shrugged. "Sometimes we do, but I thought this would be more fun."

I rolled my eyes just as another truck appeared in the driveway, this one with a bucket. "It's right there," I said, gesturing over Beck's shoulders.

"Too late," Graham called out. "I've got her."

I watched as Graham came down slowly, bouncing his feet on the tree and appearing completely comfortable with the situation. Beck expertly handled the rope as he came down. Meanwhile, Paisley climbed out of the truck and crossed over to me. "I guess they didn't need this."

"That's what I thought was happening."

Paisley shrugged. "Sorry. I was on the other side of town when Maisie called."

Graham landed on the ground, calling over, "Here she is!"

"Is she okay?" I asked as I approached him.

He had Allie's kitten, Patches, nestled in the crook of his elbow. "Right as rain," he offered.

Patches was purring up a storm. I stroked my fingers down her back. She looked all too satisfied with her situation. I held her while Graham worked with Beck to unhook himself from the ropes and get the gear put away. "Isn't she cute?" I asked as I looked over at Paisley.

She grinned. "Of course. I don't think there's ever been a kitten that wasn't cute." She cooed over Patches before stepping back. "I'll head back to town."

"Thanks for coming."

I kept a good hold on Patches, waving while

Paisley drove away with Beck following a few minutes later. After they left, Graham glanced down at me, a slow smile stretching across his face.

"She likes trees," he commented.

"I noticed," I replied dryly.

He slipped his arm around my waist, tucking his hand in the back pocket of my jeans, a habit I adored. It was a small gesture, but it made me feel like we belonged together.

It had been a full year since I moved to Alaska, and so much had happened. I couldn't even believe it had only been a year. My job was going well. My father's court case was finished, which was kind of a miracle. My father had decided to take a plea agreement rather than take his chances with going to trial. My mother was speaking to me, but that was about it. I was at peace with that for now.

I had a life here with friends, with Graham and with Allie. He startled me again and again and again. For a man who had plenty of reasons to avoid commitment, once he made his decision, he was all in.

A teeny, tiny corner of my heart wanted a ring, a formal commitment. I craved it in a strange way. Maybe because my life had blown up so spectacularly before I got here. I told myself I could be patient and wait for the right moment because we shouldn't hurry. There was Allie to consider. After I set Patches on the floor, she danced across the room, immediately aiming for this little toy that she loved bouncing around. I rubbed my hands up and down my arms as I slipped out of my shoes.

When I looked up, Graham startled me. He was waiting for me right there. "Hey," he murmured, placing his palms on the wall behind me and caging me between his arms.

"Hey."

His lips curled in that slow, sexy grin that never failed to send my belly into a swoop and a spin. Fire slid through my veins. As he looked at me, his gaze sobered.

"What?" I pressed, getting unaccountably nervous.

He lifted a hand, smoothing my hair away from my face. "I remember the first time I saw you." His voice was low and gravelly.

I was feeling all breathless as I replied, "Hard to forget. Silly girl on the highway letting her dog loose when there was a moose." I snorted. "I accidentally rhymed."

Graham chuckled and dipped his head, giving me a lingering kiss. By the time he drew away, I was near to melting like hot butter. "Thanks for rescuing Patches."

He pressed away from the wall, catching my hand in his and tugging me into the living room. We were at his house today or their house. Although we spent every night together, I technically still lived in my grandfather's old place. We hadn't had *that* conversation yet.

He stopped by the windows, looking into the trees toward the path that led to my house. "I had a whole plan," he said thoughtfully as he turned back to face me and reached for my other hand.

"Plan for what?" I prompted.

"I was going to take you out to dinner in Anchorage and ask you to marry me."

I was so startled my eyes must have practically bugged out of my head. I gasped loudly enough that Wilbur was roused from his sleep. He lifted his head from his bed, letting out a soft woof.

"Is that so surprising?" Graham teased.

"Well, um, yes," I sputtered.

He released one of my hands and reached over my shoulder to the bookshelf behind me. In another moment, he opened a small box between us. "I even got a ring."

When I looked into his eyes, I realized he was nervous. This man—this strong, tough, alpha man— looked so vulnerable, my heart felt pierced with joy and protectiveness.

"I didn't really know what to get you. I'm guessing when you were engaged before, you had something really fancy and expensive. I'm just a firefighter."

I looked up at him. "You're my firefighter, and I don't need something fancy and expensive." My throat was thick with emotion, and I didn't even realize I was crying until I felt his thumb brushing away a tear.

"What do you think?" he asked.

I finally looked at the ring. It was a platinum band. "It's perfect," I whispered.

It had a lovely pattern carved along its edge. When I looked closer, I saw that it was an infinity symbol.

"Allie helped me pick it out." His voice was gruff. "She said no diamonds because—"

I finished his sentence. "Conflict diamonds. I love that."

"I asked them to carve the infinity symbol because you're stuck with me forever."

When I looked up at him, I knew my eyes were shining with tears. "Well, that makes two of us then. I'm not going anywhere, and I love you."

Graham folded me into his arms just as the front door burst open and Allie came flying through. "Is Patches okay?"

Her words came to a stuttering stop, and then she gasped. We both looked toward her as she slapped her hand over her mouth. She started to turn away, but she spun back quickly. "What did she say?" she asked, her eyes on her father.

"I'm right here, you know," I said, laughing through my tears. "I said yes."

Allie dashed across the room, squealing as she threw her arms around us together. I was exactly where I belonged.

Want a glimpse of the future for Graham & Madison? Join my newsletter to receive an exclusive scene:
Sign up here: https://BookHip.com/RLAZSMG

p.s. If you are already subscribed, you'll still be able to access the scene.

Up next in the Light My Fire Series is Hold Me Now. Russell can't stand Paisley. And, she's his roommate, so it's impossible to ignore her. She also works with him, and a few little spats at work only leads to more sparks flying.

They discover there's one way to get rid of all that pesky tension between them and make a deal. Of course, there will be no complications, right? It's just a little lust between not-really-friends.

Don't miss Russell & Paisley's hot frenemies to lovers romance!

Pre-order Hold Me Now - due out Oct 28, 2021!

For more swoon-worthy small town romance...

This Crazy Love kicks off the Swoon Series - small town southern romance with enough heat to melt you! Jackson & Shay's story is epic - swoon-worthy & intensely emotional. Jackson just happens to be Shay's brother's best friend. He's also *seriously* easy on the eyes. Shay has a past, the kind of past she would most definitely like to forget. Past or not, Jackson is about to rock her world. Don't miss their story! Free on all retailers!

Burn For Me is a second chance romance for the ages. Sexy firefighters? Check. Rugged men? Check. Wrapped up together? Check. Brave the fire in this hot, small-town romance. Amelia & Cade were high school sweethearts & then it all fell apart. When they cross paths again, it's epic - don't miss Cade's story! Free on all retailers!

For more small town romance, take a visit to Last Frontier Lodge in Diamond Creek. A sexy, alpha SEAL meets his match with a brainy heroine in Take Me Home. Marley is all brains & Gage is all brawn. Sparks fly when their worlds collide. Don't miss Gage & Marley's story! Free on all retailers!

If sports romance lights your spark, check out The Play. Liam is a British footballer who falls for Olivia, his doctor. A twist of forbidden heats up this swoon-worthy & laugh-out-loud romance. Don't miss Liam & Olivia's story. Free on all retailers!

**Light My Fire Series**
Wild With You
Hold Me Now - coming October 2021!
Only Ever Us - coming December 2021!
Fall For Me - coming February 2022!
**Dare With Me Series**
Crash Into You
Evers & Afters
Come To Me
Back To Us
**Swoon Series**
This Crazy Love
Wait For Me
Break My Fall
Truly Madly Mine
Still Go Crazy
If We Dare
Steal My Heart
**Into The Fire Series**
Burn For Me
Slow Burn
Burn So Bad
Hot Mess
Burn So Good
Sweet Fire
Play With Fire
Melt With You
Burn For You
Crash & Burn
That Snowy Night
**Brit Boys Sports Romance**
The Play
Big Win
Out Of Bounds
Play Me

Naughty Wish

**Diamond Creek Alaska Novels**

When Love Comes

Follow Love

Love Unbroken

Love Untamed

Tumble Into Love

Christmas Nights

**Last Frontier Lodge Novels**

Take Me Home

Love at Last

Just This Once

Falling Fast

Stay With Me

When We Fall

Hold Me Close

Crazy For You

Just Us

# ACKNOWLEDGMENTS

My readers - thank you, thank you, thank you. Writing stories is a unique kind of hard work, and it can feel lonely sometimes. Also, doubt is cruel and heartless. You, my readers, carry me through those moments and somehow know just when I might need a rave review, or a kind note, or a message wondering about a certain character's story. Thank you so much for loving my stories.

Gracious thanks to my assistant, Erin. She sweeps up the details with patience and efficiency even when I forget things. Which is *a lot* sometimes.

Thank you to my editor for helping me with Madison and Graham's story. To Terri D. for catching the details I miss, some of which crack me up. Najla Qamber created a stunning first cover for this series, and I'm so grateful for her skill and patience.

My early readers help my books go out with their best grammar foot forward. Any remaining errors are mine. To the bloggers who share my books far and wide - thank you!

Last and never least, my dogs and DBC. Somehow, this book got written during a strange and trying year, and I couldn't have done it with them.

xoxo

J.H. Croix

# ABOUT THE AUTHOR

USA Today Bestselling Author J.H. Croix lives in a small town in the historical farmlands of Maine with her husband and two spoiled dogs. Croix writes contemporary romance with sassy women and alpha men who aren't afraid to show some emotion. Her love for quirky small-towns and the characters that inhabit them shines through in her writing. When she's not writing, you can find her cooking, counting the turtles in her backyard pond, and running with her dogs, which is when her best plotting happens.

*Places you can find me:*
jhcroixauthor.com
jhcroix@jhcroix.com

facebook.com/jhcroix
instagram.com/jhcroix
bookbub.com/authors/j-h-croix